Grimmtastic Girls

Cinderella Stays Late

Grimmtastic Girls

Grimmtastic Girls

Cinderella Stays Late

Joan Holub & Suzanne Williams

Scholastic Inc.

ISBN 978-0-545-51983-0

Copyright © 2014 by Joan Holub and Suzanne Williams
All rights reserved. Published by Scholastic Inc.
SCHOLASTIC and associated logos are trademarks and/or registered trademarks of Scholastic Inc.

12 11 10 9 8 7 6 5 4 3 2 1   14 15 16 17 18 19/0

Printed in the U.S.A.   40
First printing, January 2014
Designed by Yaffa Jaskoll

For you, dear reader.
We hope you
live happily ever after
every single day.

~ JH & SW

Contents

It is written upon the wall of the great Grimmstone Library:

Something E.V.I.L. this way comes.
To protect all that is born of fairy tale, folktale, and nursery
rhyme magic, we have created the realm of Grimmlandia. In
the center of this realm, we have built two castles on opposite
ends of a Great Hall, which straddles the Once Upon River. And
this haven shall be forever known as Grimm Academy.

~ The brothers Grimm

1
First Day

Twelve-year-old Cinderella clutched her school supplies and cloak in one arm as she walked down the hall in Grimm Academy. She eyed a row of lockers, looking for the one she'd just been assigned by the dragon lady in the front office. With her free hand, she flipped her long candle-flame yellow hair back over one shoulder, feeling excited and a little nervous, too.

It was Monday — her first day at the famous academy, which stood in the heart of a magical realm known as Grimmlandia. But she wasn't exactly starting off on the right foot. For one thing, she'd gotten here late. Very late. She'd missed half her classes. By now, it was almost lunch!

Her two stepsisters, who were supposed to be helping her out and showing her around the school, were walking way up ahead of her instead. Their long, beautiful dresses were made of rich blue satin that swished and swayed as they moved.

"Have you heard?" Malorette's shrill voice called out to a passing student. "A new prince is to arrive at the Academy this very afternoon! His name is Prince Awesome."

"Grimm-*mazing* isn't it?" screeched Odette, Cinda's other stepsister.

The two girls had been pretty much ignoring Cinda since her arrival at the school a half hour ago. They clearly didn't want her here. They were only showing her around now because, as usual, they were hoping she'd make a mistake. A mistake so big — even bigger than being late on the first day of school (which hadn't been her fault) — that it would get her sent home. Forever.

She shuddered. She could *not* let that happen. She absolutely had to make it here at the Academy! If she didn't, she'd wind up back home in her stepmother's clutches. A servant again. The family maid. Because ever since her dad had remarried last spring, that's what she'd become. Her stepmom was always ordering her around, and her stepsisters did, too.

As for her dad, he was sweet, but a little clueless. His fabulous new bridge-building job had suddenly made them rich last winter, right before he'd met her greedy stepmom. But his job also kept him away from home so much that he hadn't noticed what was going on. Not only that — he didn't even seem to realize that her stepmother was in fact, well, kind of evil! And so were the two Steps.

Spotting her locker at last, Cinda stopped. Carefully, she lifted the long, ornate key that hung from a chain around her neck, and turned it in the trunk's lock. "One, two, buckle my shoe," she told it softly. She felt a little odd talking to a locker. But Ms. Jabberwocky, the dragon lady in the office, had given her the key and explained that this was how the combinations worked.

Snick! Creak! In response to the rhyming code Cinda had chanted, the door in front of her opened on its own. Like all the other lockers lining the walls, this one was actually a fancy leather trunk standing tallwise instead of flat on its bottom in the normal way of trunks. It was as tall as she was and about eighteen inches wide. Its lid opened outward like a door to reveal a coat hook and three shelves inside.

"Well, aren't you excited about the idea of a new prince?" Malorette asked her suddenly.

The stepsisters had retraced their steps when they realized Cinda was no longer following them. They'd come to stand just behind her and were now nosily staring into her locker. Maybe they were hoping to find something in it that would get her in trouble, which was totally dumb. This was the first time she'd ever opened it!

"Yeah, don't you think the news is absolutely . . ." Odette

looked thoughtful, like she was searching for the most wonderful word she could think of to describe the news.

"Grimm*tastic*?" Cinda suggested.

The Steps' eyes lit up. "Exactly!" they said at the same time.

She'd tried to sound enthusiastic even though she wasn't. Because really — who cared about a new prince? Although most kids she'd seen so far weren't wearing crowns, there were plenty of princes and princesses among the Academy's students already. What made *this* prince so special?

As the other two girls discussed the prince's upcoming arrival in delighted voices, Cinda stowed her cloak in the locker, and then studied the sheet of vellum paper in her hand. It read:

Grimm Academy Class Assignments for Cinderella:
Threads
Comportment
Sieges, Catapults, and Jousts
The Grimm History of Barbarians and Dastardlies
Bespellings and Enchantments
Balls

The first two classes on the list were compulsory. Threads was probably a class about spinning, weaving, and embroidery. *Ick.*

She had no idea what Comportment was. Sieges, Cata-pults, and Jousts sounded fun, though. It was an elective — a class she'd chosen herself. Grimm History was compulsory, but at least it sounded halfway intriguing.

The last two were also electives. She was excited about Bespellings and Enchantments. She'd never done magic before and was eager to learn.

However, Balls was the class she was the most thrilled about. Would they play masketball in the class? She hoped so. It was a ball game in which players wore masks and shot balls through hoops. She was the star of her team back in the small village where she lived. *Used* to live, that is.

Cinda had said good-bye to all her friends there only yesterday, and she missed them already. What would they think if they could see her now, in this fabulous castle? Trying to act as though she belonged here.

Sadly, she hadn't gotten to say good-bye to her dad this morning. He'd been away at his new job as usual. The bridges in Grimmlandia were so old and crumbling that some were falling down. Like London Bridge. Right now, fixing it was taking up most of his attention. It was impor-tant work and paid well, she knew, but she still wished he could spend more time with her.

Brushing off her homesickness, Cinda stashed the vellum sheet, inkwell, and other supplies that Ms. Jabberwocky had given her into her trunk-locker. Then she set her book inside, too. For some reason, that dragon lady had given her only one book, even though she had six classes. And she'd just realized that all the vellum pages in the book were blank. Weird.

Right before she closed the trunk's lid-door, Cinda noticed a five-inch orange ball sitting on the floor of her locker, below the bottom shelf. *Is that a little pumpkin?* she wondered. *Did some previous student have this locker before me and leave it here?* She started to reach for it.

"Ow!" Cinda jerked around in surprise as Malorette yanked a lock of her long yellow hair.

For some reason, the Steps looked a little worried now. And all of a sudden they were in a big hurry to rush her off.

"C'mon, let's get over to the Great Hall," Malorette commanded.

"Yeah, I'm starving," added Odette. She nudged Cinda out of the way and then, after a brief pause, pushed the tall lid-door shut and stepped back.

"Me, too," said Cinda, still rubbing her head where her hair had been pulled.

"Well, come on, then," said Malorette.

Cinda turned the key again, saying, "Three, four, lock the door." She'd take whatever that orange thing in her trunk-locker was to the Lost and Found later. After classes were over, when she had more time.

Snick! Once the lock clicked into place, an image of her face magically painted itself in the small heart-shaped inset on the trunk, right above the lock.

Cinda's blue eyes widened. She wasn't used to magic just . . . happening like that.

As she withdrew the key, she looked at the trunks on either side of hers. There was a heart-shaped portrait painted on each of those, too. One of a pretty, brown-skinned girl wearing a hooded red cape. And the other of a girl with short ebony hair and a pale, rosy-cheeked face. There were heart shapes on all the trunks, she realized. They must be there to indicate who was using each trunk, er, locker.

Suddenly aware of how quiet it had gotten, Cinda looked around. The two Steps had headed off to the lunchroom without her. *Typical!* She hurried to catch up. *Clink. Clink. Clink.*

Oh, hobwoggle! She'd tried to jazz up the hand-me-down gown she was wearing by sewing some tiny bells along its hem. Major fashion error, unfortunately. Now the clinking echoed through the halls like her skirt was playing "Jingle Bells."

Malorette looked over her shoulder as she walked, giving Cinda's gown a critical once-over. "The Dark Ages called and they want that dress back," she told Cinda. Then she and Odette cracked up.

"Yeah, hello, this is the Middle Ages," added Odette. "Has been for centuries and always will be in Grimmlandia. So get it together, fashion victim."

"Thanks for the tip," Cinda replied with a bright smile. She knew it drove the two Steps crazy when she pretended their words didn't hurt her. They did, though. And after months of their continually cutting her down, she had sort of begun to feel like a loser.

Still, she couldn't resist one teeny little jab back. "It's better than being a fashion *slave*," she mumbled. She made sure to speak very quietly. Because this was the kind of thing that could land her in trouble. Something the Steps could twist into sounding way more insulting than she'd meant it to, when they snitched on her to her dad and stepmom.

"What?" Malorette demanded, turning her head to give Cinda the evil eye.

"Oh, nothing," Cinda said innocently.

Odette frowned at her in suspicion.

Cinda had promised her dad she'd try to get along with these two. But sometimes she just couldn't help herself. Besides, what she'd said was true. The Steps had fifty times more clothes than she did and wasted ten times more brainpower deciding what to wear every day. Fashion was their life — and that was okay. But what was *not* okay was the way they belittled anyone like her, who didn't really care about clothes all that much.

With a superior sniff, Malorette gave her poofy black hair a one-handed fluff, and kept walking. Odette did the same, copying her sister's sniff and fluff. As usual.

Cinda tried to shrug off their meanness by thinking about something else. Like how glad she was to be here!

Tuning out their chatter, she gazed in wonder at the inside of the magnificent turreted castle they were walking through. This was the girls' wing, at the eastern end of Grimm Academy. Classes were held on the three lower floors. The fourth floor was offices and stuff.

Her eyes found the magnificent grand staircase as they passed it. (She supposed there was a matching one on the boys' side of the school.) It branched off to lower floors and spiraled all the way up to the fourth floor. From there, a narrower and twistier set of stairs continued up to the three pointy-top towers on the fifth and sixth floors. That's where the girls' dorms were, she knew, but she hadn't been up there yet.

As she rounded a corner, she touched her fingertips to the smooth, cold marble wall. The stone's pale pink color reminded her of a winter sunrise. Maybe this marble was why the girls' wing was called Pink Castle.

The walls here were hung with tapestries showing scenes

of feasts and pageantry. And every so often, she and the Steps passed one of the tall stone support columns, whose tops were carved with figures of flowers, birds, and gargoyles.

Somewhere in this academy was the library that housed the legendary Books of Grimm, written by two brothers named Jacob and Wilhelm Grimm. The brothers had built this castle for the students who attended, but also to protect the books and other enchanted artifacts that had come from various tales and nursery rhymes they'd collected.

Just imagine! One day soon she might actually get to see those artifacts. Touch them. And read the books!

The Great Hall was a ways up ahead. Cinda had seen it from the outside this morning as she arrived at the Academy. It was a long, wide hall, with a two-story-high ceiling, that straddled the Once Upon River and connected the two wings of the Academy. Ms. Jabberwocky had told her that the auditorium and gym took up two more stories directly above it.

Beyond the Hall, the boys' classrooms and dorms stood at the western end of the school. Built of dusky gray-blue stone, their side was known as Gray Castle.

A shiver of excitement and fear swept through her. Tonight she would sleep at the Academy. And until she grew up, this would be her home. Unless, of course, the Steps succeeded in getting her kicked out!

Suddenly, Malorette spun around ahead of her. "Hello?" She stuck her face in front of Cinda's.

Cinda came to a halt, drawing back in surprise.

"Did you hear what I just said about the prince?" Malorette asked impatiently.

Cinda shook her head no. Were they still talking about that dumb prince?

"She said it won't be easy to gain Prince Awesome's notice," Odette informed her as they started off toward the Great Hall again.

"Why would you want to?" Cinda asked, walking behind them.

Odette sent her a *duh, you are beyond help* look.

Malorette muttered something that sounded like "What a pork." No, that wasn't right. She'd said "dork."

"What's the big deal about a new prince, anyway? I'm new here, too, and no one is making a fuss over me," said Cinda.

"Ha!" Malorette said scornfully. "Don't be ridiculous. Why would anyone make a fuss over you?"

Cinda let out a sigh of exasperation. "I don't *want* anyone to make a fuss over me. I just don't understand why I should be excited about another prince coming to the Academy."

"Don't you know what happens when a new prince arrives?" Malorette asked, frowning.

Two mean girls in blue dresses go gaga over him? Cinda wondered. She didn't actually say that, though. Instead she just shook her head.

"A ball!" crowed Odette. "It's an Academy tradition."

"Ball? What kind of ball?" asked Cinda. Then her eyes widened in horror and she screeched to a halt. The Steps kept on walking.

She hurried to catch up again. *Clink. Clink. Clink.*

"You don't mean . . ." she began.

Her stepsisters nodded smugly. "The dancing kind," Odette informed her.

Malorette did a cute little dance step right there in the middle of the hall. Something Cinda could never imagine herself doing without messing up.

She despised dancing and was embarrassingly horrible at it. Which was weird because she was good at sports. But dancing required a type of coordination — an ability to move to music — that was different from throwing a ball or running.

"I hope he's tall," said Malorette.

"Ooh, me, too," said Cinda.

Now it was her stepsisters' turn to look at her in surprise.

"I'm taking Balls class, remember?" said Cinda. "And every masketball team can always use a good slam-dunker."

With that, she quickened her pace and left them behind, her head held high.

Seconds later, the Steps caught up with her. "Balls class isn't about playing sports. It's dancing, fool!" said Odette.

"Wh-what?" Cinda stuttered. "But you told me it was ball *games*! Athletics. That's the reason I chose it."

The Steps cracked up again. "And you believed us? We were just joking!" cackled Malorette.

Cinda stared at them. This kind of thing was always happening. The Steps did mean things to her, then pretended they hadn't. That she'd only misunderstood. It was so frustrating!

"Still, now that you've signed up, you're going to get the new prince to fall in like with Malorette and me," Odette went on.

"Huh?" said Cinda.

Malorette grinned at her. "We did a little sleuthing and found out he'll be taking Balls sixth period. That's why we got you to sign up for it."

"Why didn't you take the class with him yourselves if you're so thrilled about him?" asked Cinda.

"Our schedules were already set, and Ms. Jabberwocky wouldn't let us change," pouted Odette. "We couldn't get a single class with him!"

"So you are going to make his acquaintance and talk us

up to him instead. You know. Tell him how wonderful we are," said Malorette. "Make him long to hang out with me. Assure him that he'll only want to partner with *me* at the ball."

"You mean with you *and* me," Odette corrected, shooting her sister a frown.

"Oh, naturally," said Malorette, but she didn't sound sincere.

Before Cinda could reply to their astounding demand, the three girls arrived at the entrance to the Great Hall. To her it seemed that all eyes turned their way. Mostly looking at her. The *new* girl. The one wearing lace-up sneakers under a floor-length, old-fashioned, and threadbare Jingle Bells dress.

What are the owners of all those eyes thinking? she wondered. That her outfit was pathetic? That her hair was tangled and her stockings dusty?

Sad, but true.

Since most of the kids in her village were boys, she'd never worried much about fashion before. But at this school there were lots of girls. And if they were anything like the Steps, they'd care more about fashion than she did. Still, she hoped she would find some friends among them. Some nice girls, not mean ones like the Steps.

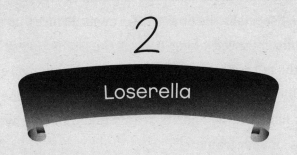

2

Loserella

The Steps swept grandly into the Great Hall, their fine blue gowns swishing. There were no clinking bells sewn to their hems. No way. Their fancy, fashionable dresses were edged with satin ribbon, just like those of all the other girls Cinda saw. And the boys in the room all wore fine tunics, with multicolored stripes and piping.

The Great Hall was every bit as magnificent as the grand staircase. There were balconies at each end, rows of windows with beautiful diamond-shaped glass panes, and colorful banners on the walls.

Cinda gaped in astonishment. She wasn't used to such luxury! Though her stepmom had redecorated their house with her dad's newfound riches, the refurbished house still couldn't come close to the majesty of Grimm Academy. And as for Cinda's clothes, well, her stepmom hadn't seen fit to buy her a new wardrobe.

As they headed for the lunch line at the far end of the Hall,

Malorette and Odette simpered and smiled at every boy they passed. Especially the ones with crowns. Princes, no doubt.

Cinda followed along behind the Steps. Every glance from those they passed made her painfully aware of the uncoolness of the gown she wore. It had been one of her mom's hand-me-downs, its seams taken in so it would fit Cinda's smaller frame.

Her heart gave a sad little thump. Her mom would have been so proud to know that she was attending this prestigious academy. But she'd died a year ago. And Cinda missed her every day.

Cinda had gone to the village school all her life. It was okay. It taught the basics. But here at Grimm Academy, she would learn everything about Grimmlandia history and magic.

Her mom had dreamed of Cinda attending the Academy. But there had been no money for her to do so until now. She knew her stepmom begrudged the tuition, but sending Cinda here was the one thing her dad had insisted on. So when a spot had opened up this term, her mom's dream had come true. Cinda wasn't going to let the Steps blow this chance for her!

Clink, clink, clink. The tiny bells on the hem of her gown tapped along the stone floor with her every step. Luckily, the sound of all the other kids' voices and the clatter of lunch trays and dishes helped drown out the bells. But not enough to suit the Steps, apparently.

"Stop that awful clinking, will you?" Malorette demanded.

Cinda lifted the hem of her long skirt so it wouldn't brush the floor, trying to quiet the bells. It helped — a little.

Even though her two stepsisters were never nice to her, she was suddenly glad to be tagging along with them. They'd been going to this academy since first grade, so despite playing mean tricks on her, they *did* at least know how things were done here.

They'd learned some magic at the Academy, too. And they'd used it against her more than once. Like the time her stepmom had told her to weed the garden back home. Every time she'd pulled a weed, another had grown instantly in its place. It had been an impossible job. Sometimes she worried her Steps might one day turn her into a toad. Or something worse!

When they finally reached the lunch line, Cinda bent to tug at her stockings, which were sagging. Then she pulled at a twig that was caught in her petticoat.

"Stand up straight! Don't draw attention to your awful gown," hissed Odette.

"Verily, you are *sooo* embarrassing," said Malorette. "Why did we have to get saddled with such a bumpkin?"

Ignoring the curious looks she was getting from other students, Cinda straightened her shoulders, pretending not to know what a mess she was. Really, it was the Steps' fault she was so untidy. They had left early in the family coach this morning, leaving her to walk to the Academy.

Which was why she'd arrived late on her very first day. It was also the reason her hair was tangled and her hem dusty. She'd had to hoof it through fields and country lanes to get here. And that was why she'd missed her first three classes already.

"Sticks and stones may break my bones, but names will never hurt me," Cinda replied softly. She forced a sweet smile as if she didn't care what the two Steps said to her. She had the pleasure of seeing them grit their teeth in annoyance.

"Names won't hurt you? Well, we'll just see about that," said Malorette.

Uh-oh! What did that mean? Cinda worried. Would she soon be croaking away and hopping up and down on a lily pad in a pond? She never should've stood up to them, even in such a small way.

The short line of students in front of them was slowly moving into an area behind a stone partition. Must be where the food was served, she guessed.

Going on tiptoe, she peeked ahead, wondering what was for lunch. She couldn't see the food. But whatever it was, it smelled delicious! Her stomach rumbled. She was hungry. Because she'd missed her ride here, she'd not only missed her first three classes, but breakfast as well.

Eventually, they made it to the head of the line. Following the Steps' lead, Cinda picked up a shiny silver tray from a stack of them. Her stepsisters each picked up a knife, fork, and spoon, and a perfectly folded white linen napkin from bins next to the trays. Cinda reached to do the same.

"Care for a bit of dessert, dearie?" a scary voice demanded suddenly. A wrinkled old hand shot into her line of vision. Its fingers held out a small plate to her. There was a three-dimensional cookie shaped like a gingerbread house on it. It looked just big enough to fit in Cinda's palm and was beautifully decorated with candies and icing.

Still holding on to her silverware and napkin, Cinda looked up into the eyes of the woman who'd spoken. Those eyes were as yellow as a cat's! And her white-gray hair was as wild and scraggly as the moss that grew at the edge of Neverwood Forest.

Startled, Cinda dropped both her knife and spoon. *Clank! Clank!* She bent to grab them as they bounced across the stone floor.

"Honestly!" said Odette, rolling her eyes. "Were you born in a barn?"

"Apologize to Mistress Hagscorch," said Malorette.

"I'm so sorry," Cinda told the lunch lady sincerely. She couldn't help it if she looked exactly like a storybook witch. And sounded like one, too.

"Don't worry your tasty, um, I mean your *pretty* little head about it," Mistress Hagscorch cackled. She pinched Cinda's cheek. Then she studied her, as if sizing up a chicken she was considering cooking for dinner.

"You're a skinny little thing, aren't you?" Mistress Hagscorch sounded disappointed, but then she perked up. "Still, I've got treats that'll fatten you up in no time."

She held out another plate of something that smelled yummy. Cinda forgot her fear of the strange woman and reached for the plate. Her hand faltered when the old crone said, "Figured you'd be tempted by my fig newts. Everyone is. How about a sour-eye scone and some of my nine-day-old pease porridge pot pie as well?"

Cinda gazed at the food. The names of everything sounded horrible. But it looked and smelled *sooo* good. Did she dare eat it?

"Uh, well . . ." she began. She didn't really want to eat anything this lady offered, no matter how good it smelled.

Clunk. Too late. The lunch lady dropped the plate of food onto her tray.

Suddenly, whispers rippled up and down the lunch line.

"Ooh! Look! The new prince has arrived," Cinda heard someone say. As she was pushed along in the line, she craned her neck to see this boy who was causing all the stir.

Malorette elbowed her. "Don't stare! Honestly, have you learned *nothing* in Comportment class?"

"I just got here, remember? I haven't been to any classes yet," said Cinda. "So what is Comportment, exactly?"

All the students near enough to hear turned to stare at her. Well, whatever it was, it wasn't taught in the village school, as her two Steps probably knew.

Odette stuck her nose in the air. "A girl with good comportment behaves in a polite and princessly manner," she said in a snooty voice. "Even if she isn't actually a princess."

"Oh," said Cinda. *The Steps must definitely have skipped that class!*

Another prince up ahead with tangled brown hair the color of swamp grass caught her eye and grinned. She grinned back.

Malorette groaned in embarrassment. "Now you've done it. Never smile at Prince Foulsmell. If you do, he'll follow you around for the rest of term like a puppy."

Cinda purposely widened her smile at the prince. Although she didn't really want to hang out with someone who smelled foul, she wasn't going to let these mean Steps tell her who to befriend.

Odette huffed at her, looking annoyed. "You're hopeless."

Just then, Malorette snapped her fingers, smirking mysteriously. "Hey! I almost forgot. There's one more thing you really need to know about this school," she told Cinda. "Our principal's health is very delicate. If you ever see him clap his hand over his mouth and look apoplectic, call out his name three times as fast as you can."

"What's his name?" asked Cinda.

The two Steps leaned in and lowered their voices to a whisper as they replied at the same time, "It's Rumpelstiltskin." Straightening, they smiled at each other in a sneaky way that made Cinda nervous.

Cinda mulled over that information as they finished getting their lunch. Once the three of them left the line, she started to follow her two stepsisters to a table. Abruptly, they stopped in front of her, causing her to bump into them.

"Uh, no, I don't think so," Malorette told her. She and Odette were shaking their heads. "You are not sitting with us."

"Yeah," said Odette. "We have an image to maintain at this school. Find a seat somewhere else, Loserella."

Cinda's cheeks flushed. After the Steps deserted her, she stood in the middle of the Great Hall. Alone. Feeling exactly like the loser they'd said she was.

Gripping her tray hard with both hands, she eyed the two long tables on either side of the Hall. Where might she be made welcome?

Anywhere at all?

3
New Friends

Cinda stood frozen in the middle of the stone floor between the two linen-draped tables. They ran the entire length of the Great Hall, one along each wall. A mix of boys and girls sat at each table, talking, eating, and laughing.

Everyone seemed to already know everyone else. Although Cinda didn't know anyone besides the Steps, she knew that these students must all be characters from literature. Just as she was. Though not all were from the books of Grimm, everyone in Grimmlandia had been brought here for safekeeping by the Grimm brothers. Cinda wasn't sure what they needed to be kept safe from, precisely. No one knew. Not really.

Through the double rows of large arched windows that stretched along both sides of the Hall, Cinda glimpsed blue skies with fluffy white clouds. Some of the windows were propped open, and birds flew in and out of the Hall, crossing in from one side and zooming back out the other.

She halfway wished she could fly away with them, back to her old happy life in the village before her dad had remarried. But she couldn't turn back time. This was her *new* life.

Spotting an empty space on a bench between two girls at one of the tables, Cinda bravely went toward it. What was the worst that could happen? If they told her she couldn't sit with them, she probably wouldn't melt into a puddle of goo. Right?

She stopped a few inches short and spoke to the girl seated on the right of the empty space. She couldn't see the girl's face at first because her back was to her.

"Is it okay if I sit here?" asked Cinda.

"Huh?" A pale, rosy-cheeked face framed with short ebony hair turned to look up at her. It was the girl from the little painting on one of the trunk-lockers next to Cinda's!

"Oh, sure. Go ahead," said the girl. She scooched over a bit to make more room. Then she started eating again. Like it was no big deal. Like she hadn't just done the kindest, most wonderful thing ever!

Grateful, Cinda set her silver tray on the table and sat down. *Take that, Steps!* she thought. *This girl doesn't mind if I sit with her and her friends. No way am I a Loserella!*

Suddenly, another girl dashed up on the opposite side of the table. She set down her silver lunch tray. *Clunk!* It was the girl in the red cape! The one from the heart painting on the other trunk-locker beside Cinda's.

"Sorry I'm late!" the red-cape girl said breathlessly. "I got turned around coming out of my third-period class and got lost." Two girls on that side of the table moved apart so she could squeeze in between them on the bench seat.

"You? Lost?" the ebony-haired girl teased gently. "No way!"

Red-cape girl scrunched her face into a goofy expression for half a second. Then she unscrunched it and laughed.

Seeming to notice Cinda staring, red-cape spoke to her. "Uh-oh. What's wrong? Is my cape askew?" She straightened it, then pushed back the hood to reveal dark, curly hair with glittery red streaks.

"No. It's just . . ." Cinda looked from red-cape girl to ebony-hair girl. "Well, I have the locker, um, trunk between both of yours. I saw your pictures in those little hearts." Using her two index fingers, she drew a heart shape in the air.

"That's weird," commented the girl on the other side of Cinda. "I mean, that your trunker would be between theirs and then you'd wind up sitting by us on your first day. It's like fate or something."

The girl who'd spoken had mysterious, dark brown eyes and long, glossy black hair. *Really* long black hair, with medium blue streaks in it. It was caught in loose, thick braids that almost touched the floor. And she wore deep red lip gloss and blue fingernail polish that was so dark it almost looked black.

Wait a minute. When Cinda sat down, the goth-looking girl's hair hadn't been touching the floor. But now it was. Had it grown an inch longer in the last few minutes?

The goth girl must have noticed Cinda staring at her hair with a puzzled expression. Because her face flushed and she immediately clammed up. Looking down at her plate, she started to eat again.

All along the table, other students were eating the odd food, too. And no one seemed to be getting sick or dying. Or even spitting it out. Cinda picked up her fork, stabbed a bit of fig newt, and nibbled. It was good!

"What's a trunker?" she said after she swallowed. "Oh, wait, I get it. Trunker because the lockers are trunks?"

Red nodded. "Mm-hmm. So you're new this term? Where are you from?"

"The village of Hey Diddle Diddle," said Cinda. At the silly name, red-cape's quick grin came and went.

After swallowing another bite of fig newt, Cinda added, "How long have you guys gone to school here?"

"Since forever. We bonded in first grade and have been BFFs ever since," said the short-ebony-haired girl.

Red-cape nodded her head toward the goth girl. "That's Rapunzel. I'm Red."

"And I'm Snow," said the short-ebony-haired girl.

"Snow's a princess," added Red. "Unlike Rapunzel and me. Luckily, she doesn't let it go to her head." She grinned at Snow.

"I'm —" But before Cinda could say her name, trumpets suddenly blared.

Ta-ta-ta-*ta*-ta-ta-*tum!*

Everyone at the table, including Cinda, jumped in surprise at the sound. She glanced up to see that two musicians had appeared on the second-floor balcony that overlooked the far end of the two-story Great Hall.

A wide, carved wooden shelf hung high on the stone wall behind them. A row of five knights' helmets forged of shiny iron sat upon it, Cinda noticed. Each had a different-colored decorative feather sticking up from its top.

Having gotten everyone's attention, the musicians lowered their long, thin, golden herald trumpets.

"Attention, scholars!" a group of formal-sounding voices chorused. "All rise for today's announcements from the great and goodly principal of Grimm Academy!"

Who is speaking? Cinda wondered. Not the musicians. Their lips hadn't moved.

The students all rose dutifully and turned toward the balcony. She did likewise.

Stomp! Stomp!

The top of a tall hat appeared above the balcony railing.

Cinda peeked at the other students around her, wondering what was going on. They were all calmly and expectantly watching the balcony.

Stomp! Stomp!

More of the hat appeared above the railing. Then a face below it. A face with a long nose and a long chin. With each step he took, a little more of the mysterious principal appeared.

He must be walking up some steps behind the railing, Cinda decided. Which was odd, because the railing was only about four feet high.

Stomp! Stomp!

Finally, the principal's head and shoulders appeared. He was a gnome! Three feet tall at most.

Strangely, his skin and clothing were splattered with brassy-colored splotches that sort of sparkled. Some of the splotches were on his arms, and others on his hat and shirt. Was it paint? Or had one of the birds flying through the Great Hall pooped on him? If so, it must have been a big bird. One with sparkly poop!

From behind her, Snow leaned closer and whispered, "He dabbles in alchemy."

"Oh," Cinda whispered back without turning around. She tried to remember what alchemy was. She was pretty sure it was the science of making something. But what?

"Greetings, scholars! Welcome to the commencement of a new year at Grimm Academy!" the principal called out. He might be small, but his voice was loud. "As most of you know, I am your esteemed and verily busy principal. So let's get on with it. This term we welcome two new students to the Academy. The first is . . ."

He held up a sheet of vellum paper and read from it. "Cinderella of *Grimm*!"

Cinda winced at his use of her full name. Like many students who went to the Academy, her family's origins could be traced to the tales of the Grimm brothers. Other students' families were linked to the books of famous authors like Andersen, Perrault, Lang, Dulac, Baum, and Carroll.

The principal's gaze scanned the crowd. His eyes narrowed with impatience. "Cinderella of Grimm, please present yourself!" he said a bit testily.

"Step out into the middle of the floor and curtsy," Red told her in a loud whisper.

"Hurry. You don't want to get on his bad side," Snow added. She flicked her hand toward the middle of the Great Hall, urging Cinda to go.

Reluctantly, Cinda stepped out from the bench. She went to stand in the center of the floor. *Clink, clink, clink.* Typical of the Steps not to warn her that this would happen!

4

Prince Awesome

All eyes were on Cinda as she executed an awkward curtsy in the middle of the Great Hall. Unfortunately, she accidentally stepped on the hem of her gown and stumbled a bit. *Clinkety. Clink.* The jingling sound was extra loud now, with everyone being so quiet.

As she rose from her fumbled curtsy, there was polite applause. And, if she wasn't mistaken, a few mean giggles from the Steps, who were sitting at the end of the table closest to the balcony.

"And secondly," the principal read from the vellum sheet, "Prince Awesome. Of the Kingdom of Awesomeness!"

A boy with dark, wavy hair rose from the table across the room. He was wearing a jeweled crown that was likely worth more than Cinda's entire village. Walking confidently to stand beside her, he swept one arm wide, then bowed low to the entire lunchroom.

Straightening, he grinned, showing perfect white teeth.

"Just call me Awesome," he proclaimed in a strong, confident voice. More applause sounded, louder this time.

Wow! He was tall. A head taller than Cinda. Or a head and a half if you counted the crown. His height really *was* awesome. Did he play masketball? she wondered. Now probably wasn't the best time to ask.

"Prince Awesome has an announcement to make," the little man in the balcony informed everyone.

"My father, the King of Awesome, has instructed me to give a ball here at the Academy!" said the prince. "In honor of my first year of attendance."

A huge cheer went up from the students.

But Cinda frowned at him, wishing she could jab him in the ribs with her elbow and stop him from saying more. Because of him and his dad, she was going to have to go to a ball? That meant she might have to *dance. Ugh.*

"The ball will be here in the Great Hall," the prince added. "This coming Friday, from eight P.M. to midnight."

"So, scholars! I recommend that you behave as good as gold all week if you wish to attend!" the principal warned them.

Gold! thought Cinda. *That's it! Alchemy is the science of making gold!* A science no one had ever perfected, as far as she knew. Otherwise, everyone would have as much gold as they wanted!

"My request for your good behavior goes for the entire

school year," the principal went on. "The great Grimm brothers" — he bowed his head in reverence to the school's benefactors for a second before going on — "built this academy and brought you all here to learn. So learn you will, or my name isn't Ruh — Ruh —"

The principal's eyes bulged and he clapped a hand over his mouth as if trying to stop something from escaping. His face turned almost as red as Red's cape. He looked like he was going to explode!

What's wrong with him? Cinda wondered. She took half a step in his direction, instinctively wanting to go help him.

But a strong hand wrapped around her arm, stopping her. She looked up into the warm brown eyes of Prince Awesome.

"Don't," he said in a low, warning tone. "Rule 37."

"What?" Having no idea what he was talking about, Cinda tried to pull away. But the prince held firm. She glanced around. She'd never reach the principal in time, anyway. Why wasn't anyone else making a move to keep him from choking or whatever was happening up there? Like those musicians, for instance. Or other students?

Suddenly remembering what the Steps had told her, she quickly yelled out his name. "Rumpelstiltskin! Rumpelstiltskin! Rumpelstiltskin!"

At her call, the prince groaned. A great gasp rose from the entire student body, filling the Hall.

The principal's face turned even redder. "Scholar! How dare you speak my name!" He pounded a fist on the railing. Then he got really cranky, stomping his feet, ripping off his hat, and jumping around like a cricket.

Cinda's jaw dropped at the sight.

"As punishment, methinks you shall do scullery duty after dinner in the Great Hall kitchen for the rest of the week!" he yelled at her. When he jumped again, he stumbled and toppled from his perch out of sight. *Thonk!*

Behind him, the five knights' helmet-heads rattled and clanked softly on their high wooden shelf. Their visors moved ever so slightly as they chorused, "She didn't know."

Those were the voices she'd heard before, she realized in amazement. The helmet-heads could speak! And whoever they were, they must be powerful, because the principal actually listened to them.

Stomp. Stomp. Stomp. He appeared at the railing again, all smiles now. "Mayhaps I was too hasty." His gaze pinned Cinda to where she stood. "You are excused from punishment. But I'll be keeping my eye on you, girl. I want no trouble, remember that!"

"Yes, sir, Your, um, Principalship," said Cinda. More giggles sounded from the Steps' end of the table. She sent a panicked look in their direction. Would they report her impertinence to her dad and stepmom?

33

The principal spread his arms wide and beamed at everyone in the Hall, suddenly in high good humor again. "I bid you farewell for now, scholars!" he called out. "And I wish you a happily-ever-after school year!"

Honestly, thought Cinda. *This principal can change moods faster than the weather.*

As he stomped down from his perch, up went the two musicians' horns again. *Whoosh!* Brightly colored flags unrolled from their trumpets' slender four-foot-long stems. In the center of each flag were two scrolly embroidered letters: *GA.* Which stood for Grimm Academy, of course!

Ta-ta-ta-*ta*-ta-ta-*tum!* blared the horns.

Once they were lowered again, the prince at Cinda's side spoke. "Your Principalship?" He was staring at her with a half-amused, half-puzzled expression.

She frowned up at him. "Well, how was I to know I wasn't supposed to say his name?" she muttered. "I was just trying to help."

He looked at her aghast. "You didn't read the handbook?"

What was he talking about? *What* stupid handbook! Feeling embarrassed and dumb for not knowing what everyone else seemed to know, she sent him a superior glance to cover up her true feelings.

"You can let go of my arm now, Your *Awesomeness*," she told him.

The minute he did, Cinda darted back to her seat. *Clink. Clink. Clink.* After a brief pause, she heard the prince's footsteps head back to the table on the other side of the room.

"Phew! That was close," Snow told her as they all sat down again. Her pale fingers were toying with the round crystal amulet she wore on the silver chain around her neck. A chain on which she'd also looped her trunker key. There was a four-leaf clover inside the amulet.

"You should never say his name," Red told Cinda. "He doesn't like it."

"I kind of figured that out," said Cinda. Which meant the Steps had set her up. Again. Now she remembered Malorette saying that she and Odette would "just see about that" when Cinda had insisted that names could never hurt her. The Steps had obviously known that saying the principal's name *could* hurt her. And it almost had!

"But *why* doesn't he like it?" she asked.

"No one knows," said Snow.

"He just doesn't," Rapunzel added, shrugging. "It makes things interesting around here, actually. We make up nicknames for him — among ourselves, I mean."

"Like 'His Principalship'?" asked Cinda.

Snow laughed. "Mm-hmm."

"Or 'Sir Stilts,' " said Rapunzel.

"Or 'Stiltsky,' " added Red.

"Or 'the Rumpster,' " joked a boy who was sitting on the other side of Red. He wore a wolf-skin jacket. There was a lean, hungry look about him. He was probably a favorite of Mistress Hagscorch, thought Cinda. After all, that lunch lady was looking for students she could fatten up!

Red sent the boy a frown, which only widened his grin. But when Red turned away from him, Cinda saw that his eyes stayed on the girl for a few seconds. Then he seemed to notice Cinda watching him, and he looked somewhere else.

"So, about Prince Awesome, Cinderella —" Red began.

"Cinda," Cinda interrupted. Then she grinned. "I'm kind of like the principal, I guess. No one ever calls me by my full name. Don't worry, though. I promise not to throw a temper tantrum if you ever accidentally do."

The others laughed at that. As everyone dug into their food, Red finished her question, asking Cinda for her impression of Prince Awesome.

Cinda shrugged. "He's very tall and he knows the school rules." Then she turned the subject to something more interesting. *Food.*

"Mistress Hagscorch can really cook," she said. "This fig newt is grimmtastic!" Unlike when she'd said that word to the Steps, this time she meant it!

Red nodded. "She's grimmazing. And generous with her recipes."

"But she's kinda scary," said Snow. "Don't you think?"

Cinda nodded. "Definitely. I'm glad those five knight heads saved me from scullery duty with her."

"Knight heads?" Rapunzel lifted a brow at her. "Oh, you mean the helmet-heads? They're the School Board. They give the principal advice and make announcements."

"And they can reverse His Stiltskinship's punishments and proclamations," said Snow.

Cinda nodded. "Lucky for me."

Just then, a ticking sound began echoing through the Great Hall.

Cinda looked toward the end of the Hall that opened to Pink Castle — the end opposite from where the principal had spoken. The sound was coming from an enormous hickory-wood grandfather clock that stood there on the balcony. There was a face on the clock's face! Eyes, a nose, and a mouth. With each tick-tock, the eyes looked left, then right. And now the mouth began speaking:

"Hickory Dickory Dock,
The mouse ran up the clock.
The clock strikes noon.
Fourth period starts soon.
Hickory Dickory Dock."

As the rhyme ended, a mechanical mouse popped out of a little door above the clock's face. It squeaked cutely, twelve times in a row, to signal the time. In the distance, Cinda heard low-toned *bongs* sounding the hour throughout the rest of the Academy.

Suddenly, the bluebirds that had been flying in the Hall dipped down to the tables. Three of them picked up Cinda's tray with their beaks. She was so startled by this that she almost squeaked like a mouse herself.

She had eaten everything on her plate, she realized in surprise. And despite the strange names, the food had made her feel kind of great. Like she'd eaten magic or something. Maybe she had!

The birds carried all of the students' trays away behind a curtain in the serving area. Within seconds, they returned. In their beaks they carried small silver bowls of water and new white linen napkins, which they set before each student. Cinda watched the others dip their fingers into the bowls and wipe them on the clean napkins. Copying their actions, she did the same.

When Snow gave the birds a few crumbs in thanks, Cinda copied this, too. Snow sent her an approving smile.

After lunch, Cinda fell into step with Red as everyone exited the Great Hall. Snow and Rapunzel were talking to each other and dropped behind them.

"Wow! I'm not used to being waited on. Especially not by birds!" Cinda told Red.

"Wait until you see what happens at the prince's ball. It'll probably be really lavish," Red told her. "I like those bells on your dress, by the way. They're grimmtabulous."

"Really?" Cinda smiled at her.

"Mm-hmm. Hey, we're going to the library to check out ball gowns after school. Want to come? Maybe you could give us some fashion tips."

Cinda almost choked. *Her? Fashion tips?* Red had to be kidding! "There are gowns in the library?" she asked, thinking it was an odd place to keep them.

Red nodded. "We can't check them out until the day of the ball. But we can reserve some now."

"Double wow," said Cinda. Actually, fashion was pretty much the lowest thing on her enjoyment list. But she would like to see the legendary Grimmstone Library. It was famous in Grimmlandia, though no one in her village had ever seen it.

Gratefully, she replied, "Sure, I'll go!"

Of course, even if she did find a gown she liked, she still had no intention of attending the ball. Because she really, truly could *not* dance! And she wasn't about to embarrass herself — *again*.

5

Pinch Me

As Cinda left the Great Hall with Red and entered Pink Castle, Malorette and Odette sidled up on Cinda's free side.

"So? Did you mention us to him?" Odette asked.

"To the prince, you mean?" Cinda asked blankly.

"No, to the moon, you moron. Obviously I meant to the prince!" hissed Odette.

"Did you tell him about us?" pressed Malorette. "We saw you talking to him when you were out there being introduced." The Steps were speaking in quiet voices, so Red and anyone else nearby wouldn't hear.

Cinda shook her head. "No, I didn't have a chance. *Ow!*" She rubbed her left side. Odette had pinched her on the ribs!

Red leaned around to see what was going on. "What's wrong?"

"That hurt!" Odette said at the same time. She was rubbing her arm.

"No kidding," said Cinda, still rubbing her side. "Why did you pinch me?"

"What? I didn't pinch you. *You* pinched *me!*" Odette said in a shocked-sounding voice. She stretched out her arm to show off a pink mark. A mark she'd made by pinching herself, of course.

"You're such a liar!" Malorette said to Cinda. "You should be ashamed of yourself. I don't know why you're so mean to us."

A crocodile tear rolled down Odette's cheek as she nodded in agreement. "We've been so kind to you. And we ask so little of you in return."

"Yet you couldn't even do that one little favor we asked," added Malorette. "Maybe you'll try harder next time?"

Red looked at Odette's pink, pinched arm. Then she studied Cinda's face with a perplexed expression.

Cinda blushed. She wasn't lying. The Steps were. But what if Red really did think she'd pinched Odette? Unfortunately, there was no way to prove that Odette had pinched *herself* to make *Cinda* look guilty.

Before Cinda could figure out what to do, Snow called Red over. Red dropped back to see what she wanted, leaving Cinda to walk alone with the Steps. If she accused them of lying, she knew they'd just act all innocent. They'd done stuff like this before to get her in trouble.

"I still don't understand why you can't just talk your-selves up to Prince Awesome," she said instead. "Why do I have to?"

Odette rolled her eyes. "Clay-brain! We can't tell him we're wonderful. That would be bragging. But when you tell him how grimmazing we are, he'll believe it." She nar-rowed her eyes to slits. "And you'd better be convincing!"

Having made their mischief, the Steps now bid Cinda good-bye with a final smirky warning.

"Fare thee well! I hope you enjoy the rest of your day," Malorette said. She used a fakey sweet voice since she was talking loud enough for others to hear now.

"Especially Balls class," added Odette. She sent Cinda a meaningful look.

After the Steps moved on, Cinda peeked over her shoul-der at Red, Snow, and Rapunzel, who were walking a few feet behind her. What should she do? she wondered.

She wanted to tell Red the truth about what had hap-pened. But it would be weird of her to drop back and start chatting with the Grimm girls, acting like she was one of their BFFs. She didn't know them that well. For all she knew, they might be friends with the Steps!

Confused and upset, and feeling lonely, too, Cinda sped off, passing classrooms on the way to her trunker. She wanted to cry and scream at the same time.

Had Red believed the Steps' lies? Would she tell Rapunzel and Snow? Would the three girls still be nice to her the next time she met them? Or would they avoid her from now on, thinking she was trouble?

Cinda didn't even know where to meet them to go gown hunting, she realized. (Or if the invitation was still open!) In the library, Red had said. But where was that? Suddenly, everything seemed too frustratingly hard. Cinda didn't know anyone here. She didn't know where anything was. She didn't really belong at Grimm Academy at all.

But she didn't belong anywhere else, either. Her house in the village didn't feel like her home anymore. Not with her stepmom changing and controlling everything.

Cinda's pity party was interrupted when a couple of boys ran past. Startled, she automatically did a little masketball move in the hallway to avoid them. *Half spin, two-step!* Realizing how silly that probably looked, she grinned to herself and suddenly things seemed a little brighter.

Hey! She wasn't going to let those Steps ruin her whole day. She wasn't the feeling-sorry-for-herself type!

Looking around, she realized she was in the wrong place. Her trunker was on the other side of Pink Castle's circular hall. Would it be faster to turn around, or keep going? She wasn't sure but decided to forge ahead.

The hall was almost empty now. Most people had disappeared into their fourth-period classes. She needed to get moving. She couldn't miss yet another class after missing the whole morning! Lifting the hem of her skirt a few inches, Cinda dashed down the hall.

Stopping by her trunker, she stuck her key into the lock and turned it. Nothing happened. She'd forgotten to say the code. She withdrew the key and started over. It seemed to take forever before it finally opened. Then she pulled out the vellum book and inkwell she'd stashed there before lunch.

Bending, she looked for the little pumpkin she thought she'd seen earlier. It was gone! Now there was only a little bit of sparkly orange dust left on the shelf. Had she seen the dust earlier and mistakenly thought it was an actual pumpkin? Maybe she'd only imagined its existence.

She shut the trunker door, said the locking code, and turned the key. Who cared about a pumpkin, anyway? She had more important things to worry about. Like getting to Grimm History class. Pronto!

About halfway down the hall, Cinda found a classroom door with a sign on it that read: THE GRIMM HISTORY OF BARBARIANS AND DASTARDLIES. This was the place!

She opened the door a few inches and peeked in at the

rows of desks. The other students were already seated two to each desk. To her surprise, half the class was boys. She'd thought guys would only have classes over in Gray Castle on the boys' side of the Academy.

Something big and oval-shaped was walking around the room, lecturing. "Grimmlandia includes the Academy, the outlying villages . . ."

When the speaker turned slightly, Cinda was surprised to see that it was an enormous egg! It was about a foot taller than she was, with arms and legs that ended in feet wearing long, pointy shoes. It wore an orange tunic and held a snazzy walking stick it tapped on the floor now and then. Was this the teacher?

At the moment, the egg's back was to the door. Maybe she could sneak in without it noticing her. She pushed the door wider and tiptoed inside. *Clink. Clink. Clink.*

Oh, hobnobbers! Those dumb bells on her hem again.

The egg turned toward her. Its shell was cracked in a few places!

"And *eggs*actly who might you be?" it demanded.

"Cinderella. Sorry I'm late. I'm new." She curtsied, stumbling a little as she did so. Just then she noticed that the teacher's name was written on the board — Mr. Hump-Dumpty.

The egg-teacher gazed at her in concern. He pointed the tip of his walking stick toward an empty space at a desk next to a boy.

"Better sit down before you fall down," he said. "Curtsies in long dresses can be very dangerous."

"Yes, sir," said Cinda. She totally agreed with him about curtsies! She slid onto the seat he'd indicated, without even glancing at the boy beside her.

"Now, as I was saying," Mr. Hump-Dumpty went on to the class. "Grimmlandia includes the Academy, Once Upon River, and the outlying villages. And Neverwood Forest. Which is so called because?"

He turned suddenly and pointed the tip of his walking stick at the boy next to Cinda. Shooting a glance at the boy, Cinda gasped. It was Prince Awesome himself! He wasn't wearing his crown now, though. She wondered if he'd stashed it in his trunker.

She stared at him as he replied, "So called because you 'never would' venture into that forest. Not if you had half a brain."

Some of the students giggled at the last part of his response, but the teacher must've agreed with the prince because he didn't scold him. Quite the opposite.

"*Egg*sellent!" Mr. Hump-Dumpty praised. He continued circling the room. "And beyond the walls of Grimmlandia, there is —" He swiveled suddenly to point his walking stick at a girl with turquoise hair, who was seated up front.

"The Dark Nothingterror," the girl supplied in a perky, bubbly voice.

"Corr*egg*t!" said the teacher.

His walking stick whipped around, and he pointed to another girl seated at the back of the room, two rows over. It was Rapunzel! Cinda hadn't noticed her in the class until just now.

Rapunzel arched an eyebrow, her expression almost daring the teacher to ask her a question. She'd seemed nice enough at lunch, but in Cinda's opinion, she dressed strangely and seemed a bit exotic and standoffish. Of course, those traits also made her very interesting, if a bit intimidating.

Cinda craned her neck a little, trying to look at Rapunzel's hair without being too obvious about it. Had it grown even longer since she'd seen it at lunch? Now it draped the floor by about three inches!

"And what is the Dark Nothingterror?" the egg demanded of Rapunzel. Apparently, arched eyebrows didn't faze him.

"A place no one has ever visited and lived to tell about it," Rapunzel replied coolly. "For terrible beasts and dastardlies are said to roam there."

"Per*fegg*tly true!" declared Mr. Hump-Dumpty. He turned and fixed the entire class with his big, worried egg eyeballs. "One must absolutely never, ever dare to sit upon the wall that divides Grimmlandia from the Dark Nothingterror," he warned. "For if someone were to have a great fall from it and land outside of Grimmlandia, all the king's horses and all the king's men could not put that someone together again!"

Cinda shivered. This teacher really knew how to put the *grim* in Grimmlandia History!

"Now, class, turn to chapter one — *Eggs*ploring Beasts and Dastardlies — in your vellum book," Mr. Hump-Dumpty instructed.

Cinda knew all the pages in her book were blank, but she set it on the desktop and opened it like everyone else was doing. From the corner of her eye, she watched Prince Awesome open his book, too. Its cover looked just like hers. As did the covers on the vellum books of the other students nearby. However, the pages inside his book and everyone else's were full of printed words.

As the egg-teacher glanced around the room, Cinda slumped low in her seat. She tried to crunch herself smaller and hide behind the boy at the desk in front of her. Unfortunately, the walking stick of doom found her and pointed right at her.

"Please read aloud," the egg requested.

"Oh, botchfibble!" Cinda murmured under her breath. Could this day get any worse? Why did he have to pick on her?

She straightened in her seat. "I'm sorry, Mr. Hump-Dumpty. I don't think I *eggs*actly —" (Oops! The teacher's way of speaking was catching!) "I mean, I don't think I *exactly* have the right vellum book. Mine's empty." She tilted it up so he could see its blank pages.

His eyes widened, causing the hairline cracks in his forehead to wrinkle. "Did you instruct it properly before class?"

"Um, no?" she said, confused.

"You have to push the button," Prince Awesome told her in a low voice. Cinda watched as he shut his book and pressed a fingertip over the oval in the very center of its cover where the scrolly, entwined *GA* letters were. "At the same time, say the name of this class," he told her.

Cinda did as he instructed. When she opened her book again, it was full of printed words about the history of Grimmlandia!

"Awesome!" she said.

"Yes?" the prince answered.

"Oh," she said, remembering that was his name. "I, uh, meant thanks!"

The prince smiled and nodded. Up close, his eyes were a super dazzling dark brown.

Cinda looked down at her vellum book and began to read aloud about the history of Grimmlandia. After she'd read for a bit, there was a discussion. Class flew by after that, and suddenly the Hickory Dickory Dock clock was announcing the rhyme time. Its deep voice was somehow being channeled through the school so that it came out of a grate high on the wall behind the teacher's desk.

"Hickory Dickory Dock,
The mouse ran up the clock.
The clock strikes one.
This class is done.
Hickory Dickory Dock."

"Please finish reading chapter one for tomorrow," Mr. Hump-Dumpty called out. "Class dismissed!"

6

Masketball

Grabbing her vellum book, Cinda rose from her seat. She glanced over at the desk where Rapunzel had been sitting. She was already gone. How disappointing! She'd hoped to say a quick hi to the mysterious girl before heading to her next class. Her reaction might have helped Cinda gauge how she now stood with the three Grimm girls after Odette's pinch performance.

Feeling eyes on her, she turned her head. Prince Awesome had stood, too, and was staring at her.

"Well, last one out of class is a rotten *egg*!" she said with a little laugh. *Toad's teeth!* Why had she said the first dorky thing that popped into her head?

For some reason, this boy was making her feel a little flustered. Which didn't make sense. She'd hung out with lots of boys back in the village — partly because not many girls her age lived there. Of course, none of the boys in the village had been *princes*. But she didn't care about crowns or royalty any more than she did about fashion! So that wasn't it.

"Where are you headed next?" Prince Awesome asked as they both turned to leave.

"Bespellings and Enchantments. Upstairs on three," she told him as he followed her through the door. Out in the hall, she said, "See you."

In two long strides, he caught up to her. "Wait, I'm going up to three, too. I'll walk with you."

She sent him a questioning look. "Until History, I'd thought guys only had classes in Gray Castle. Guess I was wrong."

He nodded, causing a lock of dark hair to fall over his forehead. With a flick of his head, he shook it back in place. "There are boy-girl classes in both towers. I've got Battle Science on the guys' side next. I can cross over on the third floor hall, past the gym."

"So how do you know so much about the Academy, any-way?" Cinda asked. "That we aren't supposed to say the principal's name? And how to open the vellum books? I mean, today's your first day, too."

One side of Awesome's mouth lifted in a half smile, and he shot her a teasing look. "Like I said before, I studied the handbook."

"What handbook?" she asked as they headed for the stairwell. "Wait! I bet I know."

Holding her book in the crook of her left arm, Cinda pushed the oval on the front of it with her right index finger. "Handbook," she tried.

Before she could check the inside of the book, Prince Awesome corrected her. "Say 'Grimm Academy handbook.'"

She tried it. After she spoke the proper title, she opened the book to find that the first page was now printed with the words:

THIS

GRIMM ACADEMY

HANDBOOK

BELONGS TO

CINDERELLA

When they reached the stairwell door, she paused to study her book for a second. At the back of it she found a list of rules. She scanned a fingertip down to Rule 37. "Never speak the principal's name," she read aloud.

Snap! She shut the book and looked at the prince.

"Thanks," she said, smiling up at him. "I wish someone had explained all this *before* this morning."

For some reason, he was just standing there staring at her again. Cinda's cheeks flushed in embarrassment and she lifted a hand to comb her fingers through her hair. She must look a sight with her wild, tangled hair and her faded, worn gown. He was so easy to talk to that she'd forgotten all about that until now.

The prince opened the door, and Cinda turned to go upstairs. "I don't know how you girls walk up these steps in such long gowns without tripping. Want me to carry your book for you?" he asked.

She shook her head, grinning. "It's an acquired knack. Back home I used to walk through fields and up steps to fetch water and carry wood for the hearth, all while wearing a long dress."

Bunching her skirts, she draped enough of the fabric over her right arm so that she wouldn't trip on her hem. Then she tucked her book into the crook of the same arm. With her free hand she grasped the stair rail. As they started up the spiraling staircase, he walked beside her.

"I had three tutors back home in the Kingdom of Awesome," the prince told her. "They helped me study the handbook and prepped me for attending the Academy. You know — the basics, like Jousting, Sieges, History, Dancing . . ."

"Oh! Dancing. That reminds me," she interrupted, remembering the Steps' demands. "Are you planning to do a lot of dancing at your ball on Friday?"

"Are you?"

"Asked you first," she said as they passed the exit door to the second floor.

"Of course I'll dance," the prince said. "That's pretty much what balls are for, so it would be rude if I didn't. And I'll ask a different girl for each dance. As my tutors schooled me was polite."

This guy sure lived by a lot of rules, Cinda decided. Still, she thought it was nice that he cared about doing the right thing. She tried to think of a way to bring up her stepsisters. Finally, she glanced over at him and said brightly, "You're probably really good at dancing after all those lessons. And you know who else is great at dancing?"

He cocked his head at her curiously.

"My two stepsisters, Malorette and Odette," she told him.

Prince Awesome looked blank.

Pausing on the stair, she held up her free hand and curved her fingers near her head. "Poofy black hair and perfect complexions? They had on matching blue gowns at lunch?"

Prince Awesome just looked blanker.

"Anyway," she said as she started to climb again. "You should make sure to dance with them at the ball. They're good dancers and they're both dying to do the waltz and reel and . . . whatever."

The prince was smiling at her now, his teeth a flash of perfect white. "Well, the Whatever is my very favorite dance, so I'll be sure to ask them," he said.

"Huh?" Was he joking? This was serious. She had to keep those Steps happy so they didn't get her kicked out of school! "Okay, um, can I count on that?" she asked him.

"Depends." He opened the door to the third floor and waited for her to go through it before him. None of the boys she knew back home would have done that. They treated her like one of the guys.

"On what?"

"On what your favorite dance is," he went on.

"Any dance I don't have to do," she said sincerely.

He laughed. "I hope I can count on at least one dance with you at my ball. We're the new students. It's expected."

Cinda sent him a horrified look as she stepped into the third-floor hall. "No way! I don't dance. It's just not my thing."

He'd startled her so much that she'd spoken much louder than she'd intended to. Her words echoed up and down the hall. Students walking nearby glanced at her with varying expressions of shock, dismay, or surprise. Apparently, not dancing was unheard of around here. She wasn't getting off to a good start at all!

But the prince only threw back his head and laughed with even more delight. "I've never met a Grimm girl who doesn't dance."

"Shh! It's actually not something I'm proud of," Cinda said in a low voice. "It's just that I'm more into sports. Ball *games* instead of ball dancing. I'm good at one and horrid at the other. So really, I'll be doing you and every guy at the ball a favor by *not* dancing."

Walking backward away from her now, the prince said, "Ball games, huh? So are you any good at masketball?"

She cocked her head to one side. "Maybe. Why?"

"I heard there's a pickup game after school in the Grimm Gym. Come if you want to." There was a smile in his voice as he teased, "If you think you can handle it . . ."

"I'll be there," she said quickly. A game of masketball was exactly what she'd need after this long and trying day!

Chuckling, he turned and headed off down a long hall she knew must go past the gym and over the river to Gray Castle. Cinda stared after him, her lips curving upward in a smile that matched his. She had to admit, that guy knew how to make someone feel pretty special. It wasn't a feeling she was accustomed to — not since her stepmom and step-sisters had come into the picture, anyway.

As she headed off to class, Cinda's smile faded a little as

she remembered something. She'd forgotten she already had plans with Red and her friends! She wouldn't be able to play masketball after all. She hoped Awesome wouldn't think she was backing out because she was chicken.

Wait a minute! What was she thinking? His tutors had probably taught him to be super charming and polite and, well, awesome, to everyone. He wouldn't care if she didn't show up. He wasn't singling her out any more than he would any other friend. Still, it had been cool of him to tell her about the pickup game after school. And nice that he'd invited her — a girl — to play with the guys. She hoped she'd get a second chance.

Her heart a little lighter, Cinda entered Bespellings and Enchantments. As she took a seat near the middle of the room, she noticed that this class was all girls.

The teacher was named Ms. Blue Fairygodmother. There was a bubble of pale blue light surrounding her. And instead of walking, she floated around the room inside the bubble, hovering a few inches above the ground. Freaky. But in a grimmarkable sort of way!

"Today's lesson is on potions and percentages of invisibility," she told the class.

Turned out that meant learning about potions you could use to make something turn a little invisible, like, say, five percent. By the end of the year, though, the teacher assured them that they'd have learned how to make things one hundred percent invisible! However, she cautioned that they must also learn some rules regarding when magical invisibility was permitted.

The class went by in a flash, and then it was sixth period. Cinda reluctantly went to the Great Hall, where Balls class was to be held. She peeked in, expecting to see people getting ready to dance. But instead, everyone was just milling around.

"The teachers aren't here," one of the other students told her.

"Teachers, as in more than one?" Cinda asked.

"There are twelve of them. The twelve Dancing Princesses. They take turns teaching, sometimes two at a time. Each one specializes in a particular kind of dance."

"They're pretty famous and give performances all over Grimmlandia. They had to leave school early today to perform at a feast in a nearby castle," another student chimed in.

A hush settled over the Hall as the School Board began making an announcement: "Attention, students! Everyone in sixth-period Balls class, please report to the Grimm Gym. You'll have gym class with Coach Candlestick this afternoon instead."

What a relief! thought Cinda. She wouldn't have to dance until tomorrow! Or maybe never, if she could talk Coach

Candlestick into switching her out of Balls so she could take Gym instead.

"Cinda, right?" a boy asked, falling into step with her as they headed for the gym.

Cinda glanced at him and nodded. He wore a small crown, and he looked familiar. "And you're Prince . . ." her voice dwindled away as she remembered who he was. Was his name really Foulsmell or was that just an unkind nickname the Steps had thought up?

"Foulsmell," he finished easily.

"So that's really your official last name?" she asked. She discreetly sniffed the air a little, making sure he couldn't tell she was doing it. She was relieved to discover that he didn't actually smell foul.

The prince nodded. "My great-great-grandfather earned it when he wandered into a den of skunks. And the name stunk, uh, stuck."

"That seems kind of . . ." Cinda had been going to say "mean," but then she stopped. She didn't want to insult his family name.

"Hey, it's all right. Could have been worse. No, wait, there's probably not a worse name, is there?" He grinned, seeming unconcerned about it. Or maybe he was simply covering up his hurt feelings like she sometimes did when the Steps teased her.

She sent him a friendly smile. "Oh, we could probably think of some. How about Prince Nosepicker? Or maybe Prince Pigfoot?"

"Ha!" said the prince, laughing with her. After that, he suggested a few hilarious nicknames, too. He was nice, she thought. A little goofy, but sweet.

"You can drop the prince part anytime you want, though," he told her. "There are so many princes here at the Academy that we usually go by our last names to lessen confusion. Which means you can just call me Foulsmell."

"Okay," she said as they arrived in the gym.

Coach Candlestick was a muscley guy who wore a whistle around his neck and held a clipboard. "Suit up if you want to play masketball this period," he told them all. When a door suddenly slammed behind him, he whipped around, looking like he expected trouble. Seeing nothing amiss, he turned back to them.

"We've also got candle jumping, putt-putt golf, quoits, tennis, and swordplay. Take your pick." Just then, someone across the gym sneezed, causing the coach to jerk in alarm.

Was he always this jumpy? Cinda wondered.

Realizing it had only been a sneeze, the coach smiled at them and punched an energetic fist in the air. "All right! Now let's get moving!"

There were two boxes on the bleachers. One was full of black masks and one was full of white ones. Cinda picked out a white one.

"I'm doing masketball," she told Foulsmell. "You?"

He laughed. "No way. I *stink* at sports! I'm going to play quoits. All you have to do is stand there and throw an iron ring at a stick. Simple." He sent her a little wave as he moved off. "Later!"

With a grin and a wave to him, she headed for the girls' dressing room, where she put on a white gym suit. Then she put on her mask and joined the other players out on the masketball court.

Everyone wore masks when they played masketball in her village, too, to indicate which team they were on. But those masks were homemade ones, cut from rough cloth. These were made of silk and satin!

And these masks must have been magical because as soon as everyone put theirs on, you couldn't recognize them anymore. Although the team members still looked like themselves, you couldn't remember who they were or if they were good players or bad ones. Which made it hard to know what their moves would be or how they'd react to your moves.

On the very first toss, the ball came to Cinda. She dribbled it down the court toward the goal. But, hey, wait a minute. Did that goal just move? She slowed in surprise. While her guard was down, another player stole the ball.

To her dismay, the game was going to be very different from back in the village. Besides not being able to tell who anyone was, the goals ran around trying to get away from the players. It was an added level of difficulty for sure. But she was up to the challenge.

The other team's top player bested her often, blocking her shots. Her sense of competition made her try harder, however, and finally she bested *him*! They went back and forth, each the stars of their teams.

The hour zipped by and suddenly a bonging sound alerted them that class was over. Everyone whipped off their masks. Cinda pushed hers upward so it held her hair back like a hair band.

"You!" she said in surprise.

"You!" said Prince Awesome at the same time. So *he* was the player she'd been trying to beat!

Uh-oh, Cinda thought. Would he be mad at her now and decide not to dance with her stepsisters? Some guys didn't like being bested by a girl.

But Awesome didn't seem to mind. "Good game," he told her, giving her a high five.

"You, too," she told him. "You've got skills!"

"So are you staying after to play pickup, too?" he asked.

Cinda shook her head. "Turns out I can't this time. I forgot I'd already promised to meet some girls in the library."

"Oh," he said. He looked like he was going to say something else, but then another guy called to him and threw the ball his way to start the pickup game. Awesome caught it. Nodding to her, he said, "Well, see you."

"Okay," she told him. As she made for the changing room, she noticed the coach nearby.

"To the left! Watch the flame!" he was yelling to a girl leaping over a large, blazing candle. He was apparently helping some students practice candlestick jumping for an upcoming competition.

The Steps had said Ms. Jabberwocky wouldn't let them switch classes. Still, it was worth a shot to try asking. She didn't care about jumping candlesticks. But if the coach agreed to switch her, she would definitely jump for joy! Cinda went over to him.

"Coach?" she asked.

He jumped a foot high, his eyes bugging out at the interruption. Seeing it was only her behind him, however, he quickly calmed again. "Yes? What is it?"

"I was wondering . . . could I switch classes sixth period? My elective is Balls, but I'd rather have Gym," she explained. "See, I play masketball and —"

"No switching except under very special circumstances," he interrupted, his eyes on the competitors. "Ms. Jabberwocky doesn't like it. And since she supplies the flame for the candlestick competitions, I don't want to get on her bad side."

Before Cinda could argue or ask what qualified as special circumstances, he went back to shouting advice to the kids jumping candlesticks. "Higher! That's the way! Keep it up and we're a shoo-in for the *Grimmess Book of World Records* in candle jumping!"

Well, at least she'd tried. Unfortunately, it looked like she was doomed to dance.

In the dressing room, Cinda ducked into the shower. She washed off the sweat from the game and the dust from the trip to school that morning, and then finger-combed her hair. Although she only had her same dress and petticoat to put back on, she looked far more presentable now. By the time she was done getting ready, it was rather late. She dashed off.

"Do you know where the library is?" Cinda asked some boys she saw, once she was out in the hall again. Ms. Jabberwocky had assumed the Steps would show her the ropes today. Ha!

"Wherever it wants to be," one of the boys told her mysteriously.

"Huh? What do you mean?" replied Cinda.

"Find the doorknob, find the library," said his friend. "All the regular doorknobs have the Grimm Academy *GA* logo on them. Look for the one that doesn't, and that's the one you use to enter the library."

"Can't you just tell me where it is?" she called after them.

The first boy shook his head. "It moves around. Could be anywhere. But I think I heard someone say it's on the girls' side today."

"Seems like a lot of trouble to get into a library," she said, heading for Pink Castle.

"It's worth it. You'll see!" he called back.

7

The Grimmstone Library

Cinda spent the next half hour searching frantically for a doorknob that didn't have the intertwined *GA* letters on it. She started on the first floor and had almost finished searching among the classrooms in the girls' castle, when she finally found the knob on the third floor.

"There you are!" she said in relief. She grasped the brass doorknob.

Honk!

She snatched her hand back and looked around. Was someone playing a joke on her? She didn't see anyone. She reached for the knob again. It snapped at her!

"Wait just a doorknobbing minute!" said a snooty voice. "Before you go grabbing someone without permission, why don't you ask if they want you to answer a riddle first?"

Cinda looked at the doorknob more closely. There was a face on it now. A goose face, with a beak. And it was talking!

"Um, I'm in kind of a hurry," she told it. "But, okay. Do you want me to answer a riddle?"

"That's more like it," said the gooseknob. "Answer me this! What do you get when you throw a gazillion books into the ocean?"

Cinda thought a minute. She'd never been to the ocean, but she had gone swimming in the lake by her village. She imagined dropping a huge bunch of books into the lake all at once. It would cause a big wave. *Hmm.* And what did books have to do with a big wave? Books had bindings, paper, words, letters, printing, and . . . *titles.*

She clapped her hands together. "I know! A title wave! Like a *tidal* wave."

Snick! Without another word, the gooseknob magically turned into a round brass knob. And a huge rectangle drew itself on the wall around the knob. It was several feet taller than Cinda and about four feet wide. A door. It was decorated with low-relief carvings of nursery rhyme characters — she recognized Little Bo Peep and her sheep right away — but she didn't take time to examine the rest of the carvings.

Quickly, she turned the knob and . . .

. . . stepped inside the biggest room she'd ever seen in her entire life. It was way bigger than a barn. Bigger than her whole village back home!

In front of her was a tall desk. There was a bell, a gooseneck lamp, and a woven basket full of goose-feather quill pens.

Beyond the desk, stretching so far into the distance that Cinda could see no end to them, were row after row of shelves and little rooms filled with who knew what. There were no windows in the library. Instead, chandeliers hung from the high ceiling, each one lit with dozens of candles.

"Hello?" called Cinda. She picked up the bell and rang it.

When no one came, she ventured beyond the desk. *Flap! Flap!* A snow-white goose zoomed by high overhead. Then another swooped in from her left side, and another flew in from her right. They were all going in different directions.

A net bag dangled from each goose's bright orange beak. Some of the bags held books. Others held objects of various kinds like, strangely enough, mittens, strings of colored lights, and a teakettle.

None of the geese paid any attention to Cinda as she walked the aisles between the rows and rows of shelving, pausing often to gaze around her in wonder. Books on every subject filled the shelves, but there was much more here than books.

There were shelves with shiny glass jars and see-through boxes containing items like watermelon seeds, toadstools, and marbles, for instance. And just about anything else you could imagine.

As she was passing between two shelves, Cinda saw an open door that led into an entire room of keys. A few aisles over was a room full of locks.

There was a room full of mirrors, too. And another one full of unicorn statues placed around a babbling brook. There was a room with a sign on the door that read: A ROOM OF IMPOSSIBLE THINGS. This room's door was shut and had no doorknob, which made it impossible to open.

Other rooms had signs that read: THE ROOM OF LOST THOUGHTS. THE ROOM OF SCRATCH AND SNIFF. Everything looked so interesting! She wished she could spend all day here investigating. All week!

If someone really wanted to, they could probably live here. Because some of the rooms were absolutely elegant, set up with chairs, tables, lamps, rugs, and wallpaper. These rooms looked like they'd been lifted out of actual houses — or fabulous castles — and dropped down into the library. There was even a room built upside down with the furniture on the ceiling. And one that was actually a cave that disappeared into blackness.

How could all this stuff fit into Grimm Academy? Cinda wondered. The library seemed as big or bigger than the Academy itself!

She watched as one of the geese swooped down and plucked a jar of jelly beans from a shelf nearby, and then carried it away in its net bag. Another goose, this one carrying a hatbox in its bag, zoomed into one of the rooms. When it flew out again, its bag was empty. Were the geese library helpers? Did they file objects and shelve books? It looked that way.

Just then, a white feather drifted down from the air to land on Cinda's skirt. She picked it up. It was a goose feather, about ten inches long, like the ones she'd seen in the basket out front, that had been made into pens.

A dark shadow fell over her and she looked up. Something huge was flying overhead. *FLAP! FLAP! FLAP!* Another goose. Only this one was as big as a horse, and someone was riding on its back!

Cinda dove to the floor as the gigantic goose came in for a landing. One of its wings nearly brushed the top of her head before it settled in the aisle.

"Well, hello. How did you get in here?" asked a voice.

Still holding the feather, Cinda sat up. The woman who'd spoken remained perched on the goose she'd been riding. She wore a frilly white cap and spectacles, and she smelled like a combination of peppermints, face powder, and cleverness. Her crisp white apron had a curlicue *L* embroidered on its front bib. *L* for Librarian, figured Cinda.

71

"I just answered a riddle and walked in the library door," Cinda explained. "I'm supposed to be meeting some friends here."

"Friends? Friends are most often filed under *F*. Hop on behind me and I'll take you to the *F* aisle," said the lady. "Unless of course —" She hesitated, then asked, "Why were you all meeting here?"

"To look for gowns," said Cinda. "Ball gowns, I mean." The minute she hopped onto the goose's back behind the woman, it whooshed off the ground again and began circling the library.

"Tell me, which is it you're looking for exactly?" the librarian inquired. "Friends or gowns? Gowns are filed under *G*."

"*G* for Gowns?" asked Cinda.

"Yes. But also for Going to balls. And for Glittery, Gorgeous, and Glamorous." She chuckled. "Or in a few unfortunate cases, Ghastly."

"So do you think I'll find my friends in the *G* or *F* section?" asked Cinda, a little baffled.

"Depends on the friend. Some are under *B* for BFFs," she was told. "Others under *P* for Pals. Still others under *L* for Loyal, *O* for Old, *N* for New —"

"Probably *N* for New," said Cinda. "Today is my first day at the Academy."

"How exciting!" the librarian exclaimed in a cheery voice. "Welcome, welcome!"

As they flew over the vast library, Cinda got a goose's-eye view of it. "I've dreamed of visiting this place. But it's way bigger than I thought it would be," she said.

The lady nodded, her attention mostly on her goose driving now. "The Grimmstone Library can make itself either small or big. Whatever it needs to be at a given moment." They swerved to avoid a chandelier, then headed down a new aisle.

"It so happens that you've come on a really 'big' day," the librarian continued. "Which means there are currently many miles of shelves. We have collections beyond anything you can imagine. The Grimm brothers acquired them and brought everything here that they believed needed protection. Music, the fountain of youth, irreplaceable documents, fantastical rooms, enchanted artifacts, mysterious memories —"

"But how does all of it fit inside the Academy?" Cinda asked, still feeling confused.

"It's magical. Movable. Timeless. Formless," said the librarian, as if that explained everything.

"Cinda! Down here," called a voice.

Cinda looked down to see Red waving to her from an aisle below. Red must not think too badly of her if she was this excited to see her. Cinda's heart lifted and she waved back.

"That's one of the friends I was looking for," she told the librarian, pointing at Red. They set down in a clear space and Red came running over, her bright red cape flowing out behind her.

The shelves around them in the New Friends aisle were filled with other items that started with the letter *N*: Nails, Newspapers, Neckties, Necklaces, Nightgowns. There was a big box labeled: NUDGES. Another box labeled: NO! And between two shelves was a door with a sign on it that read: NUMBERS.

"Hi, Ms. Goose," said Red.

"Hello, little gosling," said the librarian. She gave Red a quick hug.

So that was the woman's name, thought Cinda. Made sense. As Cinda hopped off the goose, she dropped the feather she held. It drifted from her fingers to the floor.

Red picked it up. "Oh, good. You brought a quill pen. This'll come in handy."

"Carry on, girls," said Ms. Goose. "I trust you'll remember the library rule:

To borrow an item, check it out right.
Treat it with care, and return by midnight."

"But the Prince Awesome Ball this Friday ends exactly *at* midnight," protested Red. "Do you mean we'll have to leave early to return our gowns and slippers on time?"

"Oh, you're checking out gowns for *that* ball! Why didn't you say so?" Ms. Goose adjusted her spectacles, which had slid down to the end of her nose. "The principal has magically extended the deadline for returns to the library until the morning after the Awesome Ball. Eight A.M. sharp. You can put gowns and slippers on hold now and pick them up the morning of the ball."

"What happens if we're late returning things?" asked Cinda.

"Late?" Ms. Goose raised her brows until they disappeared under her frilly cap. "You must never, ever be late." Then she lifted off, calling back to Red, "Explain the rest of the rules to your friend, will you? If you girls need me, I'll be filed under *L*."

"For Librarian?" asked Cinda.

"Of course!" said Ms. Goose. "And for Literature, Lore, and Learning, too! Not to mention Lollipops!"

Waving to the girls, the Grimmstone librarian whooshed away on her enormous goose.

"Which do you like better?" Red asked Cinda a few minutes later. They'd found their way to the *S* section of the library, and she was pointing to two different pairs of red sequined slippers. One pair had buckles and the other didn't, but otherwise they looked exactly the same.

"Well —" said Cinda. But before she could say that both pairs looked nice, Red made up her mind.

"I think I'll choose these," she said, picking up the pair with the buckles.

"Perfect," said Cinda.

"What about these?" asked another voice. The two girls turned to see Snow walking down the aisle toward them. She was holding a pair of sparkly blue slippers with perky little bows on them. "For me, I mean."

"They're cute!" said Red. Cinda nodded in agreement.

"Let's choose some for you now," Snow told Cinda.

"Shouldn't we pick out our gowns first?" Cinda asked.

"Slippers first. Our gowns will be made to match," said Red.

Picking shoes before one's gown sounded a little backward to Cinda, but she didn't say so.

Red dipped the pointed tip of the feather pen Cinda had found into a small bottle of ink that sat in a special holder on the end of one of the shelves. Then she signed her name and wrote the reservation date on the tag attached to the red slippers she'd chosen. Still holding the slippers, she left the tag on the shelf where the shoes had been.

"There's a tag attached to everything that can be

checked out of the library," she explained to Cinda. "Whenever you want to check something out, you just sign your name on the sign-out tag, and leave the tag on the shelf where you found your slippers or whatever."

As Red spoke, Cinda heard odd sounds coming from a nearby *S* aisle. *Snip, snip, snip.* Seconds later, Rapunzel appeared. Her hair was only down to her waist now. She must've found some scissors in one of the *S* aisles and used them to cut it off!

Cinda gasped in surprise. Rapunzel's hair was so beautiful. Why would she cut it? Not that it wasn't still beautiful. It was just, well, *shorter*.

At Cinda's gasp, Rapunzel eyed her a little warily. Snow and Red had shown no reaction to her shorter hair at all. Following their lead, Cinda quickly made her face a blank, pretending not to notice as well.

Rapunzel seemed to relax when Cinda didn't comment on her haircut. She even smiled at her.

Glad she hadn't accidentally said anything to offend the prickly girl, Cinda smiled back.

"Like Ms. Goose said, artifacts must be checked back into the library by midnight," Red went on.

"By midnight of the *same day* they're checked out," Rapunzel added. She started looking through the slippers to choose some for herself.

Red nodded. "With rare exceptions like the coming Ball. *Books* can be checked out for two weeks at a time, though."

"But nothing in the library can leave school grounds," warned Snow. She'd pulled the tag off the blue slippers and was using the shared pen to fill it out. After she finished, she disappeared down the Slippers aisle to place the tag on the shelf. In a flash, she was back.

"But what happens if you do return something late?" Cinda couldn't help asking again.

"Dire consequences," the three girls chorused, as though it was a line they'd all memorized.

Rapunzel picked up a pair of calf-height lace-up slippers with two-inch chunky heels. They looked more like boots than slippers. And they were black, of course. It seemed to be her favorite color.

Cinda watched her pull the tag from the black boot-slippers. Snow handed Rapunzel the pen. After she completed the tag, Rapunzel set it back on the shelf, but kept the boot-slippers.

"What sort of dire consequences?" Cinda asked. She knew she was probably being annoying, but she really wanted to know!

"It varies," said Rapunzel.

"Usually, the borrowed item's magic starts to go haywire," said Red.

"How about these?" Changing the subject, Snow picked up a pair of pale yellow slippers and held them out to Cinda.

"They match your hair perfectly!" Red told Cinda.

"Okay, I'll get them," said Cinda, nodding. The shoes were cute, but she didn't much care which slippers she chose. Because, of course, she had no intention of actually going to the ball. She signed her name on the tag quickly with the date she would pick them up as the other girls had done.

Borrower: *Cinderella*

Pickup day: *Friday*

She set the slippers back on the shelf.

"No, bring them. So we can match our gowns. C'mon," said Red. She led the way through the shelves, and the other girls followed.

8

P is for Pumpkin, G is for Gowns

On the way from the *S* section to the *G* section, the girls went through the *P* section. Cinda spotted a big empty space on one of the *P* shelves. The sign above it read: PETER PETER PUMPKINEATER'S PUMPKIN. Which reminded Cinda of the little pumpkin she'd seen in her trunker that morning. Or thought she'd seen.

"The pumpkin that goes there must be humongous!" she said, pointing at the empty place where it should've been sitting.

Red glanced at the shelf and nodded. "Big enough for Peter to put his wife inside its shell."

"Why would his wife want to be inside a pumpkin shell?" Cinda asked as they walked on.

"They're magicians. It's part of their magic act," Snow explained. "Peter Peter Pumpkineater puts his wife in a pumpkin shell. And there he keeps her very well."

"Yeah, until he makes her disappear," said Rapunzel.

"Poof!" She flicked the fingers of one hand in the air. Then she added, "Their son, Peter Peter Pumpkineater Junior, goes to Grimm Academy. He brought his parents to my Bespellings and Enchantments class on Career Day last year to talk about being magicians."

"Do you think he made the pumpkin disappear, too?" Cinda asked. "Because there's no sign-out tag on the shelf."

"When there's no tag, it means an item is only for in-library use," said Snow. "The pumpkin actually belongs to Peter Peter and is most likely on loan to the library. He must've put restrictions on it."

"Somewhere in the library right now, someone's probably using that pumpkin for a report on magical fruits and vegetables or something," said Rapunzel.

As they turned onto another *P* aisle, Cinda and Red wound up walking in front of Snow and Rapunzel. A few feet ahead, Cinda spotted a box labeled PINCHES. Her eyes met Red's, and she could tell that Red had noticed it, too.

Cinda's cheeks turned pink. Unable to help herself, she blurted, "I didn't pinch Odette."

"I know," said Red. "She pinched herself."

Cinda stared at her in surprise. "You knew?"

"I figured it out. What I didn't figure out is why she wanted me to think you had done it."

With a shrug of one shoulder, Cinda looked away. "We just don't get along."

"What are you guys talking about?" asked Snow as they continued on.

"That box of pinches we passed," said Red.

Cinda was glad when Red left it at that. She didn't want to talk to them about her problems with the Steps. Even if this was the *P* section, where Problems probably belonged!

When they finally arrived in the *G* section, Cinda's companions kicked off their shoes. They put on the slippers they'd chosen for the ball, so Cinda did, too.

There was a tiny mirror, no bigger than a three-inch square, hanging in the middle of a large, otherwise empty wall at the end of the aisle they were in. With thumb and forefinger, Red, Snow, and Rapunzel each tugged on the corners of the mirror's silver frame and gently pulled outward at the same time.

To Cinda's amazement, the mirror began to stretch, getting bigger. In no time at all, it was taller than they were and wide enough so that all four girls could stand before it and see their reflections.

"Why is a mirror in the *G* section?" asked Cinda.

Red tapped her fingernails on the mirror. "Glass," she explained. The rapping seemed to wake the mirror, and now it spoke:

"What do you wish?
You need only to ask,
And I will complete for you
Any fair task."

Red replied:

"Mirror, Mirror on the wall,
Please make us gowns for Prince Awesome's ball."

"Mine should be made of red satin with a big velvet bow around the waist," she went on. "Oh, yes. And velvet sleeves." She gestured with her hands to indicate how she wanted the dress to look and fit.

When Red was done, Snow stepped forward a little. "I'd like one that's pale blue with a wide skirt, and sleeves to my elbows," she said. "And some sparkles here and there." After she spoke, she stepped completely away from the mirror so it wouldn't show her reflection anymore.

Noticing Cinda's curious glance, Snow murmured, "Mirrors weird me out."

"Black, please," Rapunzel told the mirror next. "Long sleeves that go all the way down past my wrists onto my hands. Scoop neck. And a narrow skirt with a slit up to one knee. No sparkles."

"Oh, come on," begged Snow. "Sparkles are fun!"

"Okay," Rapunzel said, quickly giving in. "Add sparkles. But only around the neckline."

The three girls all looked expectantly at Cinda now. "Your turn," said Red.

Although Cinda didn't know the first thing about designing ball gowns (if she had, she wouldn't have sewn bells to the hem of the gown she had on), she closed her eyes and tried to imagine the prettiest dress she could think up. Then she opened her eyes and described it.

"It should be yellow to match my borrowed slippers. Scoop neck, with puffy sleeves and a full skirt." She looked at Snow and grinned. "And sparkles, of course!"

"Sounds adorable," Snow said in a happy, dreamy voice. She was obviously really into fashion.

Suddenly, there came the sound of dozens of small flapping wings. Bluebirds were flying toward the girls from across the library. Probably coming from the *B* section, Cinda thought.

Their beaks were hanging on to bedsheet-size pieces of fabric, which billowed out behind them like colorful sails. There was a bright red piece, a soft blue piece, a black piece, and a buttery yellow piece.

The birds dropped down beside each girl and got to work. They wrapped Cinda in the yellow satin cloth. The color matched her candle-flame hair exactly. More birds followed, overlaying the satin skirt with see-through yellow fabric.

"Shouldn't we take off our other gowns first?" Cinda asked the others. "My hem's a little dusty."

"Don't worry," said Red. "It'll be fine."

"Okay." Cinda trusted her new friend to be right.

Snip! Snip! Pairs of birds opened and shut little silver scissors. They darted here and there, working two by two to snip away fabric where it wasn't needed.

As Cinda's dress began to take shape, the old one she was wearing underneath magically faded away. She was startled to feel it disappear. Ms. Goose had said they couldn't take the ball gowns from the library today. So what was she going to wear when they left?

With threaded needles in their beaks, some of the birds began sewing. Others flitted around, chirping at the stitchers, as if offering them fashion advice in birdspeak.

Minutes later, all four girls stood before the mirror again to admire their finished, elegant gowns. Ribbons were tied just so and the tiny sparkles on their bodices and skirts winked in the chandeliers' candlelight from overhead.

"Wow!" Cinda said softly. She turned from side to side, studying herself in the glass and enjoying how the skirt of her gown swayed and swished. The color and style were exactly as she'd imagined and described them to the mirror. She looked, well, beautiful!

Longing filled her. It really was too bad she wouldn't actually get to wear the gown. No way was she going to that ball, though. She'd make a fool of herself if she had to dance. She'd just have to come up with some excuse to get out of going.

"We'd better hurry," said Red. "I think I hear some other girls coming. They'll want to use the mirror to make their ball gowns, too."

The minute Cinda took off her new gown, her old one reappeared. So it wasn't gone forever, after all. Which was definitely a good thing, since she couldn't very well walk around the Academy in her underwear!

The girls quickly hung the new gowns on a long, empty rack and tagged each one with their names and the date they would pick them up. Cinda had to admit that this visit had been fun, even if she wasn't quite as much into fashion as her companions. Trying on new outfits could be surprisingly entertaining with cool girls like these, who weren't always critical like the Steps.

They all took off their chosen slippers and placed them in net bags as Rapunzel waved over some geese flying above them. Four flew down, took the bags in their beaks, and flapped away with them, heading for the *S* section where the slippers would stay until they were picked up on Friday.

Since the girls were still in the *G* section, Cinda asked, "Are the Great Books of Grimm here in this section, too?"

"Sure, want to see them?" asked Snow.

"Yes!" Cinda said excitedly.

A few turns later, they were inside a room lined with bookshelves and stuffed with things belonging to the Grimm brothers. Dozens of portraits hung on one wall, including seven in carved golden frames that were grouped together in the center. For some reason, one of those seven was covered with a drape so the painting couldn't be seen.

Cinda's eyes went wide when she noticed that objects were moving around the room under their own power. A deck of cards shuffled itself and then settled onto a polished antique desk in four even piles. An umbrella in the corner leaped upward, opened, twirled around, and then shut itself again.

"It's the most magical room in the library," murmured Red.

"In the whole of Grimmlandia!" Snow agreed.

When a swan-shaped paperweight lifted from the desk and headed Cinda's way, she started to duck. But it seemed to know she was there, because it circled around her and gradually came to rest on a shelf.

A sign on that same shelf read:

Protected here are the writings of the
Grimm brothers, Charles Perrault,
Hans Christian Andersen, L. Frank Baum,
Lewis Carroll, Andrew Lang, Edmund Dulac,
Mother Goose, and other great works of
fairy tale, folklore, and nursery rhyme.

"Ms. Goose is an author?" Cinda asked in surprise.

The others nodded.

"Rhymes are her specialty," said Rapunzel. "She thinks up most of the trunker combinations we use."

"Hey, I'm getting hungry," said Snow. "Is it okay if we head out now and come back some other time? We don't want to be late for dinner!"

"Sure. Thanks for showing me all this." As Cinda followed the three girls to the door, she glanced over at the ornate desk, where the cards were now flipping themselves face up in some kind of game. Above the desk hung a splendid coat of arms, which looked like a big shield with various gold emblems on it. Probably it was the Grimm brothers' coat of arms, Cinda thought, since most everything in this room related to them.

As she stared at the shield, something changed. All at once, a small, roundish area of the coat of arms went misty and foggy. Transparent, almost!

And then . . . what was that . . . was there a nose showing through? Cinda blinked. When she looked again, an *eyeball* seemed to peek out at her through the hazy circle of mist.

"Eek!" Cinda shrieked. *Clinkety. Clink. Clink.* The bells on her hem jingled wildly as she dashed from the room. Spooked by her outburst, the other girls sped up, too.

When they were all back out in the hall again, Red asked her breathlessly, "What was that about?"

"I saw . . . I mean, I thought I saw an eyeball peeking out of that coat of arms by the desk! Just for half a second. Then it disappeared," said Cinda.

"Good," said Snow, looking freaked out. "I mean, it's supposed to be a coat of arms. Not a coat of eyeballs!"

When the other two girls exchanged looks that seemed skeptical, Cinda was instantly sorry she'd said anything. Did they think she was lying? "Maybe I only imagined it," she said quickly.

It had been a *very* long day, after all. And she wasn't used to magic. Maybe the novelty of it was messing with her head!

Pearl Tower

As they left the library, the girls heard the Hickory Dickory Dock clock bong nine times. "Nine o'clock!" said Cinda. "How did it get to be so late?"

"Oh, no, we missed dinner completely!" said Snow. "Time flies in the library," she explained to Cinda. "Once I was in there for ten hours, and thought it was only ten minutes."

"Time can also drag in there, though," said Red. "Back in first grade, I got lost and thought two days had passed, but it only turned out to be two hours."

Rapunzel nodded. "Never knowing how the hours are passing can make it hard to get things checked back in on time!"

The Grimm girls headed up to the twisty stairway that led to the three dorm towers.

When they reached the door to the stairs, Rapunzel opened it for the others, but she didn't go up. "Night," she told them softly. Then she turned back the way they'd come to head down the grand staircase again.

Where was she going? Didn't she sleep in the dorm tower, too? Cinda wondered.

"Wait. I'll go with you," Red called to Rapunzel. "We can stop by the kitchen and ask Mistress Hagscorch for some leftovers. You can take some, and I'll bring some up to the tower for Cinda, Snow, and me."

"Okay." Rapunzel paused on the stairs until Red joined her, then they went down together.

Watching the two girls go, Cinda looked at Snow with a question in her eyes.

"Rapunzel sleeps in the dungeon," Snow explained matter-of-factly.

"But why?" Cinda asked as the two of them took the stairs upward. Then she remembered how mad the principal could get. "Is she being punished?"

Snow shrugged. "No, nothing like that. It's just that heights make her dizzy. And nervous. Or going up the stairs does, anyway. She's okay going down stairs. But getting her up to our dorm is a challenge. After all, it's in the highest part of Grimm Academy. So that's a lot of stairs to go up!"

"Oh. Poor Rapunzel. Do you know why she's so afraid?" asked Cinda.

"Nuh-uh." Snow's ebony hair bounced as she shook her head. "She can be a little touchy about the subject, so we pretty much leave it alone."

Fearing heights when you lived in a towering castle had to be hard, Cinda thought. There was no way to avoid stairs. Fortunately, she felt totally different from Rapunzel about going up. It didn't bother her at all — in fact, excitement filled her as she followed Snow higher and higher.

Eventually, the stairs dead-ended at two doors on the sixth-floor landing. One was emerald green and one was pearly white. Snow opened the white one. It led to an outdoor stone walkway that ran between the towers.

"You're over in Pearl with Red and me." Snow spoke in a quiet voice since it was getting late and some girls might be sleeping with their windows open. "The Pearl Tower dorm, I mean. I saw your name on one of the sleeping alcoves in there this morning."

Outside, the night was cool and the sky was a dark, velvety blue. Cinda heard splashing and looked over the side wall of the walkway. Below them in a courtyard between the fifth-floor dorm towers stood a tall, three-tiered fountain. Far, far below that, starlight danced like diamonds on the Once Upon River.

Above their heads, the pointy top of Pearl Tower gleamed a pale, frosty white. The top of the tower they'd just left was a sparkly green, the other a dazzling red.

"All the towers have jewel nicknames," Snow went on. "The ones on our side of the Academy are Pearl, Ruby, and Emerald."

"What are the boys' towers called?" asked Cinda.

"Onyx, Topaz, and Zircon. Your stepsisters are in Ruby Tower," Snow added. "You could probably trade with someone there if you want to be closer to them."

"No, that's okay," Cinda said quickly. No way did she want to be near the Steps. In fact, hearing that the Steps weren't assigned to her tower made Cinda want to do a jig. Almost. If she hadn't despised dancing.

At the far end of the outdoor walkway, they came to another pearly white door. They went through it and entered the sixth-floor Pearl Tower dorm.

Inside, the circular dorm was ringed with what Cinda realized must be little bedrooms. Each one had a decorative curtain as an entrance, but no actual door.

In the center of Pearl Tower was a common area, where girls could gather. It had space with a fireplace hearth that was so tall she could've stepped inside it without hitting her head. Surrounding the hearth were a dozen or so comfy chairs, a few tables, and a bunch of throw cushions on the floor. One table had a game board set up on it.

"You're over here," said Snow. She showed Cinda to one of the curtained alcoves. There was a tasseled silk sign pinned to the curtain with two names embroidered on it in swirly black calligraphy letters. The first name was Mermily. The second was Cinderella.

"Go on in and get settled. I'll get some dishes out for when Red brings food. Come to the common area when you're ready," Snow told her.

"Okay, thanks," said Cinda. She pushed back the curtain and peeked into her alcove. Not seeing her roommate, she stepped inside. It was a cozy room with a cute oval-shaped rug lying in the center of the floor. Directly beyond the rug on the far wall was a big window.

On either side of the window and rug were two beds. They were canopy beds with swooping swags of pretty see-through fabric draped across their tops. But Cinda had to really crane her neck to see the canopies because both beds were raised about six feet off the floor on tall bedposts!

At the end of each bed stood an armoire with mirrored doors. Cinda opened the one closest to her. There were dresses hanging inside it already, so she quickly shut the armoire door. The girl named Mermily must have already claimed this side of the room.

Mermily's bed had a coverlet decorated with wavy turquoise lines that made Cinda think of the sea. But where was that girl, anyway? She was out late for a school night!

As Cinda crossed to the other side of the room, she noticed that someone had made up her bed, too, with a pale yellow coverlet. There was a desk beneath each bed, and she was relieved to see her small trunk from home sitting under her desk. A coachman had stowed the trunk in the carriage with the Steps' luggage that morning. And an academy servant must have brought it up here.

Her little trunk contained her only other two dresses, clean underthings, and her hairbrush. And something else even more precious. She kneeled beside the trunk and opened it. At the top she found what she wanted. A flat, square bundle. She carefully unwrapped it and pulled out the small, framed picture of her mother.

"I'm here, Mom. At Grimm Academy! Can you believe it?" Cinda whispered. She gave the picture a quick kiss, then set it on top of the desk. Her stepmom had forbidden her to bring the only picture she had of her dad. Instead, the cruel woman had given that picture to the Steps to put in their dorm room.

Not wanting to dwell on her stepmom, Cinda wandered over to the armoire at the end of her bed and peeked inside. A pale yellow nightgown and robe were hanging on hooks. And a pair of fuzzy matching house slippers had been neatly placed at the bottom of the armoire. Courtesy of the Academy, she concluded. How nice! These things were far finer than any of the clothes she'd brought.

Just then, she heard the stairwell door open and shut. A few minutes later, she heard the clinking of dishes and smelled the delicious aroma of food. *Mmm!*

Cinda parted her room's curtain and followed her nose.

As she, Red, and Snow ate the snacks Red had brought, a few of the other girls who lived in the dorm came and went. Cinda met one named Goldie, and another named Pea. And others whose names she didn't quite catch, but which she was sure she'd learn soon.

The three Grimm girls were all hungry, so they wolfed everything down in no time. Soon they wished each other good night and went to their alcoves to go to bed.

Back in her room again, Cinda yanked off her dress and tossed it in the bottom of the armoire. She'd wash it when she got the chance.

There was a ladder at the end of each girl's bed since the beds were so high up. Cinda quickly climbed her ladder, and then flung herself onto the mattress. Ooh! It was unbelievably comfy. Before her dad had made his fortune, her mattress at home had been made of prickly straw. And in the summer, there were sometimes fleas.

But this bed was as soft as a cloud. Its sheets smelled of a spring meadow. Practically purring, Cinda snuggled in. So far, things hadn't gone half bad. She was making new friends and it was only her first day at the Academy! She just hoped the Steps would stop pestering her about Prince Awesome and quit trying to ruin things for her.

She was too tired to worry about them for long, though. So tired that she fell right to sleep in her petticoat!

10

Home Sweet Hearth

*C*inda woke the next morning to the sound of voices. She rubbed her eyes, yawned, and stared up at the ceiling. Her shared alcove was open to the top of the tower. Through her bed's gossamer canopy, she could see the shimmering pearly white of the inside of the ceiling, which rose to a point high in the center above the common room.

The voices came again. They were speaking in harmony. Loud harmony. It was those School Board knights. They were making an announcement that was somehow being channeled through the whole school. She listened as they repeated it a second time.

"Will Jack and Jill please bring a pail of water to the front office? There's a small fire. Nothing to be concerned about. Carry on, students."

"Fire?" Cinda echoed to herself. She frowned and sniffed the air, a little worried. Accidental fires were common in her village, where most homes were made of wood and mudstraw.

But Grimm Academy was built of stone. Fires seemed unlikely. There was some wood, she supposed, remembering the dining tables and the shelf the five helmet-heads of the School Board sat upon. And she did smell smoke. Alarmed, she sat up.

Just then, the Hickory Dickory Dock clock rang out the rhyme time. It was seven o'clock.

On the last stroke of seven, the turquoise-haired girl from her Grimm History class walked into the bedroom. Cinda hadn't heard her come in last night but knew it must've been late.

Yet she was already up, earlier than Cinda, and she must have showered, since she was dripping wet. The girl was dressed in a turquoise robe that had the *GA* letters embroidered on its breast like a logo. She smiled at Cinda.

"Hi. I'm Mermily," she said in that bubbly voice Cinda remembered from class. She started towel-drying her hair, which reached to her waist. "You're Cinderella, from my History class."

"Mm-hmm, but call me Cinda."

As Mermily nodded, Cinda pushed up on one elbow, looking down at the girl from her high bed. Her long, tangled yellow hair fell forward into her face. "So there's a fire somewhere?"

"Sounds like it," said Mermily. "Smells like it, too."

Cinda flipped her hair back over one shoulder. "Aren't you worried?" she asked. "Shouldn't we, like, leave or something? I mean, if the castle might burn down?" She scooted to the foot of her bed, toward the ladder.

"It's no big deal. Principal Rumsy dabbles in alchemy, you know. And Ms. Jabberwocky breathes fire to heat things when she helps him with his experiments. Sometimes things go a little awry."

If Mermily expected that information to somehow calm Cinda's worries about the school burning down, it didn't! Mermily didn't seem upset, though. She began digging around in her armoire for something to wear. She pulled out one of the dresses Cinda had seen in there last night.

Cinda glanced at the other bed in the alcove. It was already made up again, its coverlet neat and tidy. "Wow! You must get up early. I usually do, too. But I was tired last night. Yesterday was a looong day."

Mermily grinned and rolled her eyes. "I totally understand. First days usually are. Still, you'd better get moving if you want to get breakfast in the Great Hall before class. Washroom's four alcoves down. Look for a door instead of a curtain. Everything you need is there. Towels, soap, shampoo."

"Thanks." Cinda climbed down the ladder and took the robe from the hook inside her armoire. She put on the fuzzy slippers and stepped through the alcove curtain. She sniffed the air again. The smell of smoke was fading, so the fire must be under control. Good thing!

She headed for the washroom. Inside, it was divided into private shower compartments. Everything was so luxurious. Marble walls and floors. Gold faucets. *Grimmazing*, thought Cinda, feeling dazzled. Back home, she'd bathed and washed her clothes in the stream!

By the time she returned to her room, Mermily had left for breakfast. Cinda pulled out one of the two clean dresses she'd brought in her small trunk and put it on. She wished she'd thought to hang it in the armoire last night. Oh, well. Nothing she could do about the wrinkles now.

When she stepped into the common area again, Red and Snow were just exiting alcoves that were several curtained doors apart. Cinda had assumed the two were roommates, but obviously she'd assumed wrong.

"C'mon," Red called to Cinda. "We're meeting Rapunzel in exactly two and a half minutes."

Together, the three girls scurried down five flights of stairs and over to the Great Hall. Once there, they went through the breakfast line.

The very second they sat down at one of the long tables, it began snowing! No, wait. It wasn't snow, Cinda realized. Instead, little pieces of paper were fluttering down from overhead, appearing out of nowhere to land on the tables.

One of them dropped onto Cinda's silver tray, barely missing her saucer of pears. She picked up the slip and read it aloud. "Hearthkeeper." She looked at the others. "I don't get it. What's that supposed to mean?"

"It's your tower-task assignment," Red told her.

Cinda's heart sank, just a little. Back home, her step-mom had made her a servant. Cleaning the hearth had been her least favorite job. And now she would have to do it at the school?

"Can we trade assignments?" she asked quickly.

Everyone within earshot looked startled at the very idea.

"No!" said Snow. "The slips choose us at the start of every year. They know who is best suited to a task."

When a slip of paper landed in front of Red, she picked it up eagerly. "Yes!" she exclaimed, pumping her fist in the air. "I got Snackmaker!"

Snow grinned at her. "You always get that." She looked at Cinda and confided, "Lucky for all of us in Pearl Tower — because Red makes the best cookies ever!"

Just then, Snow and Rapunzel got their chore assignments, too.

"Tidy-upper," said Snow. She smiled, appearing pleased. She did seem like the kind of person who'd be good at keeping things tidy, Cinda thought, remembering how Snow had brushed up the bread crumbs and fed them to the birds.

"I got Fountainkeeper!" Cinda heard her new roommate, Mermily, say from a couple of benches away.

Rapunzel looked at her slip and tucked it into her pocket without saying anything.

Wondering what Rapunzel's assignment could possibly be since she didn't actually live in the dorm tower, Cinda read her own slip again. Cleaning a hearth was dirty work. She was disappointed that the slips considered such a job right for her, but she would do her best.

After they'd all finished breakfast, the two musicians blared their horns again and the principal came to the balcony to make morning announcements.

"Students of Grimm Academy!" he began. "I have disturbing news. There's been a theft from the library!" At this, a gasp sounded from everyone in the Hall.

"A roundish, orange object has been taken. An object owned by Peter Peter Pumpkineater. It's the size of a very, very small house. One that a wife could fit inside. It also inspired a nursery rhyme penned by Ms. Goose herself. Can you guess what it is?"

The answer is obvious, thought Cinda. *A pumpkin.* But since no one else was volunteering the answer, she didn't, either. No way she wanted to chance scullery duty by speaking when she shouldn't and getting on the principal's wrong side again.

The Rumpster looked rather pleased when no one shouted out the answer. "It's a pumpkin!" he exclaimed. "If anyone has any information about this theft that could help us find the culprit, please make haste to the front office!" Having finished what he'd come to say, he stomped back down his stairs.

As the students left the Great Hall and headed for their first-period classes, everyone was buzzing about the principal's news. "Wow! So that's why that space in the *P* section was empty yesterday," said Snow.

"I bet Ms. Goose is *honking* mad about it," said Red, as the four Grimm girls walked together toward their classes.

Listening to the other girls discuss the theft, Cinda wasn't quite sure what to do. Should she tell them she'd seen a pumpkin in her trunker yesterday? Or thought she had seen it, anyway? Until it disappeared? That sounded dumb even to her.

They already seemed to think she was imagining things, like that eyeball in the Grimmstone Library yesterday. Would the principal think the same thing if she told him? He'd said he didn't want any trouble out of her.

Red and Snow were talking about lunch plans now. Cinda opened her trunker. Still no pumpkin inside. Even if she *had* actually seen it in here yesterday, it had been way too small to house a wife. So it couldn't possibly be the one belonging to Peter Peter Pumpkineater, right? Must be just a coincidence. Feeling relieved, she grabbed her vellum book and went on her way.

It turned out that Red was in her first-period Threads class, too. There were two teachers, Ms. Muffet and her helper, Ms. Spider. Exactly as Cinda had feared, they were going to be doing projects in spinning, weaving, and embroidery, plus sewing and needlepoint.

When she poked her finger with the blunt needle for the third time, she sighed. "I don't really get the *point* of needlepoint," she told Red. Which earned her a look of shock from Ms. Muffet and Ms. Spider. Stuff like needlepoint was probably their life!

Ms. Spider came to sit beside her. Her eyelashes were long and black and her dress was overlaid with fine cobwebby-looking lace. "Let me see if I can help," she told Cinda kindly.

But before Ms. Spider could give her any helpful hints, the School Board began to blare out an announcement. "Attention, students! Will Red, Rapunzel, Snow, and Cinderella please report to the front office?"

As everyone in class turned to look at Red and Cinda, they traded a look of confusion and, well, *panic*.

"Uh-oh," said Red. "This can't be good."

11

Grumpystiltskin, Troubles, Classes

As Cinda and Red headed for the principal's office on the fourth floor, they met Snow and Rapunzel.

"What do you suppose we've done wrong?" asked Red as they climbed the stairs.

"No idea," said Snow.

"Don't look at me," said Rapunzel. She gripped the stair railing tightly and took careful steps as she went upward.

"Me, either," said Cinda. "Maybe we weren't called in because we're in trouble. Maybe we've won an award or something." She knew it was wishful thinking. After all, what award could she possibly qualify for after only one day at school?

The other girls didn't answer, which Cinda took to be a bad sign. Wasn't anyone ever called to the principal's office for a happy reason?

When they entered the office, Ms. Jabberwocky — the dragon-lady assistant — was at her desk. Cinda had been in this part of the office to get her supplies and trunker code yesterday. But beyond Ms. Jabberwocky's desk stood a door marked: PRINCIPAL R'S OFFICE.

Ms. Jabberwocky rose and smiled at the girls, showing enormous, sharp dragon teeth. Using two fingers, she picked up a jalapeño pepper from a plate on her desk. Then she tilted her head back and opened her jaws wide.

She tossed the pepper up into the air and it dropped into her mouth. After munching it, Ms. Jabberwocky washed the pepper down with a big glug from a bottle of hot sauce.

"O frabjous day! Callooh! Callay! We've been expecting you," she told the girls. When she pronounced the letter *p*, a bit of fire sputtered out of her nostrils. Probably the reason the office smelled faintly of smoke.

Ka-boom! Suddenly, there was a small explosion from behind the principal's door.

"Bandersnatch!" Ms. Jabberwocky shouted in alarm. "Follow me, Grimmble girls!" She dashed into the principal's office.

"Does she always talk nonsensically like that?" Cinda whispered to Red as the girls reluctantly followed the dragon lady.

Red nodded. "You get used to it. After a while, it even starts to make sense!"

Principal R's office was full of equipment and stuff. So full, the girls had to go single file at first. The shelves on either side of them held strangely shaped dark lumps that Cinda decided might be really bad art sculptures. There were also jars of gold-colored flakes, a tank of swimming goldfish, a vase of goldenrods, and a picture of a golden retriever.

Red pointed to one of the darkened lump things. "Gold-making experiments gone wrong," she whispered to Cinda.

So that's what the lumps were! Now that she thought about it, they did look sort of toasted. Which made sense, with Ms. Jabberwocky being Principal R's assistant and all.

As the girls moved past the shelves, they saw the principal's desk. Sitting empty behind the desk was a large throne with the *GA* logo carved into its high back.

Clang! Clang! Cinda looked over and saw the principal banging a hammer against what looked to be a large lump of coal. He was standing at a heavy-duty metal worktable and wore an outfit like the blacksmith's back in her old village — a big square iron mask, sturdy gloves, and a black apron.

All around him, there were more lumps. Some burnt-looking and some not. One of them was as big as Cinda. Was it a student? Had Principal R gotten mad at some poor girl or boy and turned her or him into almost-gold?

Ignoring the girls, he went on hammering. Even Ms. Jabberwocky seemed to have temporarily forgotten them. Suddenly, Principal R shouted, "*Now*, Ms. Jabberwocky!" On command, she took a quick swig of hot sauce from a bottle nearby and snorted out a long stream of fire at the coal lump.

When Ms. Jabberwocky was through, the principal picked up the charred thing in his gloves and turned to the girl nearest him. Which, unfortunately, happened to be Cinda.

"Does this look like gold to you?" he demanded.

She gulped, but said truthfully, "Not really. It looks more like coal with some metal stuck to it."

Behind him, Ms. Jabberwocky had been waving her hands and shaking her head, trying to get Cinda to be more encouraging. To say that maybe it did look like gold. But Cinda hadn't noticed the signals until it was too late.

"Dagnabbit! I was afraid of that," said the principal. He tossed away the blackened lump and stomped over to his throne. There were stairs on one side of it, leading up to the seat. He went up them. *Stomp. Stomp. Stomp.* Then he hopped over the arm of the throne and sat, looking mighty grumpy. But at least he didn't seem to be mad at *her*, Cinda thought. *Phew*.

"Have a wabe, girls," Ms. Jabberwocky told them. She smiled as if nothing were amiss. Since the other girls immediately sat on three of the four chairs facing the desk, Cinda figured *wabe* must mean "seat" in Jabberwocky-speak. So she sat, too.

The shelf behind the throne held dozens of books about alchemy. Cinda saw titles like *You Can Strike It Rich* and *Treasure Can Be Yours*.

Yet the throne itself looked as if it were made of real solid gold! And the school was full of expensive things like silver and tapestries. So why in Grimmlandia would the principal care about striking it rich? Cinda wondered. She didn't dare ask, though. He might tell Ms. Jabberwocky to breathe fire and turn her into a lump of almost-girl, almost-gold!

"Let's get down to business," Principal R said now. "Where is it?"

"Where's what?" Rapunzel asked after a few seconds of no one saying anything.

"Peter Peter Pumpkineater's pumpkin, of course. A little goose told me you girls were in the library yesterday in the *P* section. You must have stolen it. I want it back."

"We didn't steal it!" Cinda exclaimed. At the same time she was thinking, *The geese can talk?* The other girls protested along with her.

Principal R raised an eyebrow. "So it just grew legs and ran off on its own?" He hopped from his throne onto the top of his desk and began pacing back and forth, glaring at each of them in turn as he passed by their chairs. "Come on, which of you is the pumpkin rustler? We cannot have unauthorized thieves in this school."

Did that mean that authorized thieves were okay? Cinda wondered. *Weird!*

Hic! Hic! Snow looked really nervous. So nervous she had started to hiccup.

The principal stopped in his tracks. "Those are guilty-sounding hiccups, scholar. You stole the pumpkin, didn't you?" He pointed an accusing finger at her.

"No, *hic,* no, I did, *hic,* not!" protested Snow. "I'm allergic to fruit!"

A pumpkin is a fruit? thought Cinda. She'd thought it was a vegetable.

Principal R rounded on Snow. "Then who did? I —"

"Wait!" said Cinda.

The principal whipped around and stared hard at her. "You're that new girl. The one who dared speak my name. Well? What do you have to say for yourself?"

Cinda took a breath for courage, then more words spilled from her lips. "I saw a pumpkin in my trunker yesterday. It was little, though. Far too small to fit a wife in."

The other three girls looked at her in surprise.

"It was there when I first opened the trunker before

lunch," she blabbered on. "But when I opened it again after lunch, the pumpkin was gone and I haven't seen it since."

"Aha!" the principal hollered gleefully. "I knew it! I knew you were hiding something. Peter Peter Pumpkineater's pumpkin is magic and can become any size or shape. Certainly small enough to fit in a trunker."

"Oh. I didn't know that," murmured Cinda. "I guess that means the one in my trunker could have been his. But I didn't steal it. And I'm sure Snow didn't, either! Honest."

Surprisingly, Principal R didn't seem all that mad at her. In fact, he seemed happier now. Happy that he'd guessed correctly? Was that all that mattered to him? Guessing right when others couldn't? (Or when they dared not!)

Still, she wished she'd gotten around to saying something about that pumpkin sooner. At least to the other Grimm girls. Because she hadn't, she knew she sounded guilty now. Would she be punished? Maybe even banished? Sent home to a house with an evil stepmother who treated her like a maid? Expecting the worst, she awaited the principal's next words.

But he only continued pacing back and forth across the desktop, muttering to himself and seeming to forget the girls for a moment. "Appearing and disappearing without rhyme or reason. Hmm." He paused, looking very worried, and then went on. "This comes at a bad time. A very bad time. Peter Peter Pumpkineater's pumpkin contains the

Seeds of Prosperity. Which means the school will fail to prosper. Unless we find that pumpkin again, we'll have to tighten our belts."

He stopped and glanced at the girls as if he'd just remembered they were there. He gave them all a big fake-looking smile. "Never mind all that. I don't want you Grimm girls worrying unnecessarily. I'll take care of things. I've got a secret plan to set things right."

"Does it involve making gold?" Cinda couldn't help asking.

The principal's eyebrows rammed together. "How did you guess?" he demanded. He began twirling around his desk in circles, suddenly hopping mad. Coming too close to the edge, he accidentally whirled right off the desk onto the floor. *Thonk!*

While he was still down there, unharmed but red in the face, Ms. Jabberwocky called out quickly, "Visit is over, girls!" She ushered them out of his office in a hurry.

"Never ever try to guess his secrets!" Rapunzel whispered to Cinda as they approached Ms. Jabberwocky's desk again.

"It puts him in a bad mood," added Red.

"He's always grumpy, but I've never seen him this bad," said Snow.

However, it seemed to Cinda that a bad mood was his *usual* mood. In fact, she decided that her own private nickname for him would be Grumpystiltskin!

"Mmm. Well, I'd better get back in there," Ms. Jabberwocky told the girls. "I know he seems mimsy crabby, but it's with tulgey good reason."

"The missing pumpkin?" asked Cinda. She hoped everyone believed her when she said she hadn't stolen it.

"That's the least of his slithy tove worries," said Ms. Jabberwocky. "He's up against a manxome foe." She clapped a hand to her scaly forehead. "Pay no attention. I've said more than I should. Run along." Waving them off, she shooed them out into the hall.

Once the office door had slammed behind them, Cinda turned to the others. "Even if I were a thief and I wanted to steal something, I wouldn't steal a pumpkin. Why would anyone bother with a pumpkin when there are riches everywhere you look in the Academy?"

She gestured along the walls of the hallway to marble and gold statues, crystal chandeliers, and jade ornaments. "And why is Principal Grum . . . I mean, Principal R working so hard to make gold anyway? Can't he just sell a few things off if the Academy really needs money?"

"Not allowed," said Snow. "Rule 8 in the handbook."

"Cinda's right, though," said Red as they headed down the hall. "Something weird is going on."

"Ms. Jabberwocky mentioned a foe," said Rapunzel.

"Who could it be?" Cinda wondered aloud.

Nobody had an answer.

But Snow looked at Cinda and said, "Thanks for standing up for me in there."

"Yeah, it was really sweet of you," added Red.

Rapunzel nodded.

Their approval meant a lot to Cinda. She was glad her new friends seemed to accept that she had nothing to do with the pumpkin's disappearance. Like her, they just wanted to figure out what was going on!

As they reached the stairs, the Hickory Dickory Dock clock bonged. Time for second period.

A voice called her name. "Yoo-hoo! Cinda!"

Cinda looked over her shoulder and saw the Steps coming down the hall toward them. Malorette was waving at her, and Odette was right behind her.

"I'll see you guys later," Cinda told the other Grimm girls. After Red and the others left, the Steps caught up to Cinda.

"So. Have you made any progress?" Odette asked.

"With the prince," added Malorette.

"I have!" Cinda said truthfully. "Turns out that Prince Awesome is in my History class. And I did mention you to him."

"How exciting!" said Odette, bouncing on the toes of her slippers.

"Tell us exactly what you both said," said Malorette. "Every word." She gave Cinda a nudge and they all began to move down the winding stairs together.

Cinda tried to remember. "Well, I told him you were in the Great Hall yesterday when he and I were introduced to the Academy."

"Did he notice us?" Malorette asked breathlessly. "Did he say we stood out like no others?"

"Um, he wasn't sure," Cinda hedged. "But I described how you looked. Blue dresses and black hair. I mentioned that you were both good dancers. And that since he was probably good, too, he might want to ask you to dance."

"Excellent use of flattery. Boys like that," advised Odette.

"But don't pour on the flattery too much. He might fall in like with you instead of us," said Malorette. Then she looked at Odette and they both burst out laughing, as if the very idea of his liking Cinda was a hilarious joke.

Cinda's cheeks grew warm. So what if she didn't dress as well as they did or have perfect princess manners?

That didn't mean she wasn't as worthy of a boy's attention as they were. Besides, even if she did say so herself, she'd looked pretty in that yellow dress yesterday. Anyone could look nice if they could afford to. Or if they had access to magic!

Suddenly, she'd had enough. She came to a screeching halt halfway down the stairs to the next floor. "You know what? If you want to flatter the prince, you can just do it yourself because I —"

Malorette paused and turned to eye her. "Interesting about that missing pumpkin. I wonder what Principal Stiltsky would think if we mentioned we saw it in your trunker yesterday?"

Cinda gasped. "I already told him about that. But how did you know —? I mean I wasn't sure I'd — wait! Are you the ones who stole it?"

"How dare you accuse us!" huffed Odette. "We saw that pumpkin in there when you opened your trunker. You're lucky we didn't rat you out, thief."

"Thief? No! I wasn't the one who put it there." She and the Steps started to move again as other students came up behind them on the stairs. "I'd only just arrived at the Academy," Cinda insisted.

"Uh-huh. So you say." Malorette looked bored and

pretended to study her nails, which were painted a bright green to match her dress.

When they reached the landing, they pushed through the door to enter the circular hall. "It would be a shame if we had to report to our dad that you were called to the principal's office for theft!" said Odette.

They'd been doing sneaky things like this ever since Cinda's dad married their mom. Things to gain her dad's favor and turn him against her. It made her so mad that they were calling him their dad. He was her dad first! She would have been glad to share him. But they were trying to take him away from her. And now they were trying to frame her for theft!

"If I talk you up to the prince, will that be enough? Will you unsteal the pumpkin? Return it to the library? And promise not to tell my dad about my visit to the principal's office?"

"Stop blathering on about that pumpkin," said Malorette as they started down the hall.

"Besides, if we had stolen it, you can be sure it would be for a good reason," said Odette. Malorette shot her a frown, shushing her.

"What's that supposed to mean?" asked Cinda.

"Just make sure Awesome dances with us at the ball," said Malorette. "Do that, and your secret is safe with us. Ta."

With fluttery waves of their fingers, the two girls took off toward their classes. They'd made it sound like Cinda actually *was* the thief and they were covering for her! Ooh! They made her so mad!

It took Cinda a minute to realize she'd followed the Steps too far and was on the first floor, instead of the second, which was where her second-period Comportment class was, so now she turned around and went back up one floor.

She was a few seconds late by the time she found the right classroom. From the doorway, she could see the teacher sitting behind a desk draped with a pink linen tablecloth. There was an elaborate place setting on it, and the teacher was talking about it. Was today's lesson something about dishes and silverware?

The teacher's name was written across the board at the front of the room: *Ms. Queenharts of Wonderland*. Fittingly, her dress was covered with white, pink, and red hearts, and she wore a small red crown.

Stepping inside the classroom, Cinda shut the door quietly behind her. She tried to edge her way to a seat without drawing the teacher's attention. But naturally she didn't succeed.

Ms. Queenharts aimed her laser-beam eyes in Cinda's direction at once. "You're late, young lady!" she announced in a dramatic voice. "Off with your head! Off with your head!"

With her left hand, Ms. Queenharts picked up a heart-shaped muffin from the table. In her right, she held a silver butter knife. *Whack!* She sliced off the frosted top of the muffin. Cinda's eyes widened in shock.

"Take a seat! Take a seat!" yelled Ms. Queenharts.

Cinda scurried to a chair. It looked like Ms. Queenharts's temper was almost as bad as Principal Grumpystiltskin's!

Although she survived the class without *actually* losing her head, Cinda still thought Ms. Queenharts was weird.

Next period — Sieges, Catapults, and Jousts — turned out to be way more fun. It was held on the lawn outside Gray Castle, where they practiced lobbing hay bales with catapults. Cinda's made it all the way from shore to the dead center of Maze Island, which was in the middle of Once Upon River!

The rest of the day flew by, and then it was time for the most dreaded class of all — Balls. Unfortunately, there was no escape this time.

Her class was made up of ten girls and ten boys, and was held in the middle of the Great Hall. Ms. Twelve, the youngest of the Dancing Princesses, was their teacher today. Her specialty was flamenco, a Spanish dance that involved lots of clapping and stomping. It was beautiful when *she* did it, and most of the students grasped it quickly. Especially Prince Awesome.

Unfortunately, Cinda couldn't catch on to the beat. Every few minutes, the students changed partners. Soon, she'd stomped on the feet of almost every boy in the class. Most were now eyeing her warily.

"Just think of it like a masketball game," Awesome suggested to Cinda when it was their turn to be paired together. "You're dancing your way to the goal."

He did a little example of what he meant, acting as if he were flamenco-stomping his way to make a shot. Cinda laughed, her tension fading a bit. But then they all changed partners again, and she was paired with someone else. As Awesome danced off with another girl, he called back to her, "Relax. The object is to have fun."

"Ow!" said Cinda's partner as she tromped on his toes.

"Sorry," said Cinda. Despite Awesome's coaching, this was not her idea of fun! By the time they left the Hall, more than one boy was limping. And it was all her fault!

12

Hearthkeeper

Two nights later, Cinda was in Pearl Tower staring at the hearth in dismay. It was full of ashes from the fire that had burned there the last few days. Time to clean it. Much like dancing, this was *definitely* not her idea of fun.

She dug around in the common area closet and found a straw broom. It was pretty scraggly. But the minute she wrapped her hands around its handle . . . *whoosh!* The broom took control!

It began twirling and whirling her around the common room, causing her to trip and stumble over pillows and bump into tables. It must be magic! That was kind of cool. However, it wasn't being very helpful as far as cleaning went.

"Ow! Whoa! Hold your bristles, broom!" she begged. It didn't listen. She tried to let go of its handle, but her hands seemed stuck to it. After one full circle of the room, the broom whirled back to the hearth and finally got down to business, sweeping and sucking up the ashes like a vacuum.

Wow! Back home, it had taken an hour to sweep the hearth. But the work was a snap with a magic broom! After a few breathless minutes of effort, the hearth was spic-and-span and the broom calmed down. Finally able to let go of it, Cinda quickly tucked it back in the closet and shut the door.

Phew! Feeling slightly dizzy, but relieved to be finished with her chore, she went to her room to study.

Once seated at her desk, Cinda pressed the button on the cover of her book. "Comportment," she said. Then she opened the cover.

Her understanding of the subject grew as she began to read. Comportment was about etiquette, which was the same as good manners. Only in Cinda's opinion, Ms. Queenharts didn't have any of those. So maybe she meant for her students to learn to do the opposite of what she did?

Cinda rubbed her forehead. School here was confusing. She'd hoped to be around magical stuff and learn magic herself. But now she was halfway wishing that the teachers and studies would be more normal!

There was a knock on the wall outside her curtain and then Red's voice called to her. "Come look what your room-mate has done!"

Shutting her book, Cinda leaped from her chair and followed Red to the outdoor walkway that Snow had led her along on her first night at the Academy. They leaned way out to gaze down to the big fountain in the middle of the fifth-floor patio below.

There were now two mermaid statues atop it! Suddenly, the bigger one moved. It wasn't a statue at all!

"Is that — Mermily?" Cinda whispered in surprise.

Red nodded. "She's a mermaid. Didn't you know?"

Cinda shook her head, gazing at her roommate in wonder. Instead of standing on her usual legs, Mermily was balancing on an iridescent blue-green tail in the water that filled the smallest, topmost ring of the fountain. She was holding a fancy-looking wrench, and had added a mermaid statue about half her own size to the center of the fountain's top tier. It was curved in the shape of an *S* and spurted water in three streams that looped over each other to fall into the lower rings of the fountain.

"It's grimmtacular!" Red called down to her.

"It really is!" Cinda agreed.

Mermily smiled up at them and gave her tail a happy splash. "Thanks! Since I'm Fountainkeeper this term, I thought I'd shake things up a bit. Get creative."

"Hey, Grimm girls!" a voice called just then.

Cinda and Red looked over to see Awesome, Foulsmell, and two other boys Cinda didn't know. They were outside playing putt-putt golf on the long narrow courtyard that ran the length of the flat rooftop above the auditorium.

Below the auditorium was the gym, and below that was the two-story-tall Great Hall. Taken together, they all formed the four-story building that spanned Once Upon River between Pink Castle on one end and Gray Castle on the other.

When the girls waved back, the boys started making silly shots, showing off for them and making them laugh. Cinda wished she could join their game. But she had more homework — a History test to study for.

For the last two days during History and Balls class, she'd been talking up the two Steps to Prince Awesome as much as possible. Only, he kept changing the subject. For some reason, he wanted to know stuff about the village Cinda came from, her old friends, and her hobbies.

What would the Steps do if he didn't pay attention to them at the ball? Try to get her in some kind of big trouble, that's what! Tomorrow was Friday, the day of the Awesome Ballsome, as everyone had nicknamed it. She still wasn't planning to go. But she had no idea how she was going to get out of it.

It wasn't until the next morning that a brilliant idea presented itself. It happened when Cinda awoke to another School Board announcement.

"Attention! All students must complete their assigned tower tasks or they will not be allowed to attend tonight's ball. Knights in armor will be posted at the door to the Great Hall to ensure that all who are admitted to the ball are in compliance. For further details, refer to Rule Number 75½ in the handbook."

Cinda bolted upright in bed. *That was it!* The perfect excuse. Like Mermily, she would "get creative" with her tower-task assignment. She would mess up the hearth so that she'd have to stay late to clean it. She'd make sure that the mess was something the magic broom couldn't fix. Something that couldn't be sucked up and would take a while to clean. Soup, maybe. She'd seen some stored in the cabinet in the common room. Perfect! And that would be her reason for not attending the ball!

After breakfast, she, Red, Snow, and Rapunzel picked up the gowns and slippers they'd reserved in the library. They were getting ready to head back to their rooms when Cinda spotted the Steps coming down the stairs toward her. The other three Grimm girls continued on, unaware of the drama that was about to unfold.

The Steps' eyes went to the gown Cinda held. It was mostly covered with a cloth for protection, but bits of yellow satin peeked out at the neckline and hem. Would they demand to see her gown and then make fun of it? She spun around, hoping to escape them —

And walked smack into Prince Awesome! Cinda moved

left to go around him, but he moved left, too. He moved right to get out of her way, but she moved right, too.

The prince laughed. "Hey, Grimm girl, I guess you know how to dance, after all! Be sure to save me one at the ball tonight." His eyes went to her ball gown. "I'll watch for Cinderella dressed in yella!" With that, he went off down the hall, still grinning at her over his shoulder.

Meanwhile, Odette and Malorette were standing on the stairs, watching the whole "dance" thing. And they did not look happy.

They stalked out into the hall and up to Cinda. "You haven't been talking to him about us at all, have you?" Malorette accused.

"All this time, you've been flirting with him yourself. Hoping he'll dance with you instead of us!" Odette hissed.

"No," Cinda began. "I hate dancing! You know I do."

"Humph," scoffed Malorette. "But you like princes, apparently."

"You'll be sorry," said Odette. Again, her eyes flicked to the dress Cinda was holding.

Cinda was fed up with their threats. But before she could gather the courage to tell them so, they pushed past her and kept walking. Frustrated, she gazed after them, trying to calm herself down.

She was starting to like it here at the Academy. Yelling at them wasn't worth the risk of getting sent back home. She'd just have to try to keep out of their way from now on. Another reason to avoid the dance. Once they discovered she wasn't there, and once Prince Awesome gave them each their one dance apiece, maybe they'd leave her alone!

Sixth period was canceled that day so the Hall could be decorated for the ball. There wasn't a sit-down dinner in the Hall, either. Instead, Mistress Hagscorch made take-out newt dogs on buns, which everyone ate in the Bouquet Garden, picnic-style. Snow and Red spent the whole time trying to convince Rapunzel to join them in the Pearl Tower dorm to get ready for the ball.

"It'll be more fun that way," Snow insisted.

"We'll be with you every step of the way up," Red promised.

Finally, Rapunzel agreed. But she looked even paler than usual at the thought of going six floors up!

After dinner, Cinda watched as Snow and Red each took one of Rapunzel's arms, gently encouraging her up the stairs. They didn't seem to notice when Cinda held back. Which made her feel a little left out. It was obvious how much the other three Grimm girls all liked and cared about one another. They were nice to Cinda, but she wasn't one of their BFFs. How could she be? She'd only been here four and a half days!

Cinda split off from the other girls and ducked into an empty classroom. Feeling sort of lonely, she did some home-work, waiting for time to pass. When she heard the Hickory Dickory Dock clock bong seven P.M., she went upstairs. The ball would start at eight.

By the time Cinda reached the dorm, all the other girls were already zipping around, getting spiffed up. Most of the curtain-doors were open so everyone could help every-one else get ready.

She heard Red calling to someone about perfume. Mermily was over in another girl's alcove, helping her choose the perfect color of lip gloss. Rapunzel had obvi-ously survived the trip upstairs, because she and Snow were helping fix each other's hair. By now, Rapunzel's hair had somehow grown long again. It was all the way down to the floor.

Making sure no one saw her, Cinda slipped into her alcove and slid the curtain shut. It was now or never. Quickly she changed into her old pj's from home, not wanting to take the chance of totally ruining one of her three old gowns.

Checking that the coast was clear, she tiptoed over to the common room in the middle of the dorm, planning to "accidentally" spill some soup on the hearth. A mess just big enough to keep her busy while everyone else attended the ball without her. But when Cinda got to the hearth, she gasped.

Because it was already a disaster! Someone had dumped the lentil soup from the cabinet and a bunch of blueberries, too, all over the hearth! With enough time, she could clean up the soup, but how would she ever get the stains from the berries out of the stone?

"What in the grimmworld . . . ?" Cinda heard someone murmur. She glanced around to see that some of the other Pearl Tower girls had gathered close without her noticing, including Red, Snow, and Rapunzel. They were all in their petticoats or robes, not yet fully dressed for the ball.

"Who did this?" Red asked.

"I don't know," Cinda said truthfully. But almost instantly, she realized who the culprits had to be. Who else but the Steps! They'd told her she'd be sorry. Of course, they'd had no idea she'd been planning to make a similar mess herself to avoid attending the ball. Still, this was much worse, and it made her hopping mad that they had done something so mean.

The hearth was beautiful. It was her job to take care of it. And they'd probably ruined it forever!

"Be right back," Cinda told the others. Forgetting she was in her pj's, she tore out onto the walkway and stormed over to Ruby Tower. Cinda wasn't sure what she was going to say to the Steps or what she'd do, but she had to let them know she was onto them. Being mean to her was one thing, but what they'd done had hurt everyone in Pearl Tower. For once, she wouldn't stay silent and let them get away with their evil deeds!

The Steps' names were embroidered on their alcove's curtain. It was closed, but Cinda could hear the two of them talking inside. Before she could call out to them or pull the curtain back, she overheard something that made her ears perk up. The word *pumpkin*. Huh? She put her ear to the curtain, listening.

"The pumpkin is in position for the big rollout," said Malorette. "No thanks to Cinda, who had to go and get assigned the very trunker where it was hidden in the first place."

"Don't worry," Odette replied. "She has no clue about the rollout. Much less that tonight's ball will create the perfect magical conditions for it to occur."

"Right. If all goes as planned, the E.V.I.L. Society will be pleased with us," said Malorette. "Especially if we also succeed in recruiting Prince Awesome. We absolutely must dance with him tonight and talk him into joining."

Evil Society? What was that? Cinda wondered. It definitely sounded bad!

And it also sounded like the Steps knew way more about Peter Peter's pumpkin than they'd let on. And that they were plotting some kind of dastardly deed with it that would take place during the ball. How unfair! Even if Cinda didn't want to go, everyone else at Grimm Academy was *so* looking forward to this event.

And what about Prince Awesome? Why would the Steps want to ruin his ball? Or get him to join an evil society? She thought they liked him!

Suddenly, the curtain whipped open. The Steps stared at Cinda in surprise. They were both dressed in costly matching gowns made of rose-colored satin. As Malorette fastened the laces at the front of hers, she pulled the chain holding her trunker key from around her neck and tossed it onto her bed. For some reason, her key was white instead of iron like everyone else's.

Before Cinda could speak, the Steps looked her up and down and started laughing.

"Pj's? Good choice to wear to the prince's ball," Malorette said spitefully.

"Yeah, since you don't like dancing, you won't have to worry. No one's going to ask you, looking like that!" said Odette.

Blushing a little, Cinda folded her arms and glared at the girls. "Someone messed up the Pearl Tower hearth."

Malorette smirked. "Well, you're Hearthkeeper for your dorm, right? I guess you'll have to clean it up. Which means you won't be able to go to the ball tonight."

"Oh, that's too bad," Odette said in an insincere voice.

"You did it," said Cinda. "I know you did. You dumped lentil soup and strawberries on that hearth."

"You mean blueb —" Odette started to correct her.

"Hush!" said Malorette. But she was too late.

"Aha!" said Cinda, flinging her arms wide. "You did make that mess! How else would you know it was blueberries, not strawberries?"

Malorette's smirk widened. "Prove it." Then she whipped the curtain shut, leaving Cinda out in the hall.

"Well, don't think you're going to get away with your evil pumpkin plan tonight!" Cinda called to them.

The curtain whipped open again. The two girls stared at her, looking worried now.

"You were eavesdropping!" said Malorette.

Cinda narrowed her eyes at her. "Prove it!"

Turning on one sneakered heel, Cinda stalked off to the stone walkway and hurried all the way back to Pearl Tower. She was going to go to that ball after all, she decided. Just to spite the Steps. And to foil their plans, whatever they were. But first she'd tell the other Grimm girls what she suspected. And then she'd clean the hearth as fast and as best as she could!

When she entered her dorm, Red, Snow, and Rapunzel were still crowded around the hearth. They had opened the closet and gotten out the broom, a sponge, and a bucket. It looked as if they were planning to clean up.

"No!" said Cinda. "I'll do that. It's my job. Though I don't know how I'll ever get those berry stains out."

"I do!" Snow held up a spray bottle and grinned. Her tower task was Tidy-upper, Cinda remembered.

"Is that some kind of magic cleaner?" Cinda asked hopefully.

Snow nodded. "Flour, hydrogen peroxide, and some other magic stuff I mixed up. It's great for getting stains out of stone."

"Let's get started on this mess," said Red.

"But —" began Cinda.

"We insist," said Snow.

"With all of us working, you'll get to the ball sooner," said Rapunzel.

Cinda looked at her friends, hardly able to believe what they were offering. Because she really did want to go to the ball now. To stop the Steps from executing their wicked plan!

"Thank you," she said softly. "You guys are the best!"

"Pearl Tower Grimm girls stick together!" said Red.

"Yeah! Pearl Tower power!" said Rapunzel, punching a fist in the air.

As they got to work, Cinda told the others what she'd overheard her stepsisters saying. Her friends were as worried as she was, but none of them exactly understood what the Steps were plotting.

Just as the school clock bonged out eight o'clock, the girls turned from the sparkling hearth. With Snow's cleaner and all four girls sharing the task, they'd finished in no time.

"Last one ready is a rotten Mr. Hump-Dumpty!" called Red. Giggling, they all dashed to their alcoves.

When Cinda opened her armoire, she found her yellow ball gown crumpled at the bottom of it. Why wasn't it still on the hanger she'd hung it on that morning? she wondered. She picked it up and drew in a sharp breath. Her beautiful gown had been destroyed! Its skirt was slashed and its bodice ripped apart. Even the yellow slippers were torn. The Steps! They must've done this, too!

Now all she had left were her three ugly dresses from home, her cloak, her pj's, and a robe! No way the knight guards would admit her if she wore those. None of the other girls in the dorm would have a spare ball gown just sitting around in their armoire either. What was she going to do?

And what would Ms. Goose say when Cinda showed her the slashed gown? She had borrowed it, so she was responsible for it. A magic-mirror-designer gown was probably expensive. How could she possibly pay for its loss?

After throwing her old cloak over her pj's, Cinda grabbed her tattered dress and torn slippers and went in search of the others. But when she pushed her curtain aside, they were just arriving in their ball gowns to get her.

"Wow! You look grimmazing!" she told the other three Grimm girls. And they did.

Snow looked adorable in her blue dress. She had dusted on a hint of blue eye shadow and had wrapped a blue satin ribbon in her hair and tied it into a cute bow.

Meanwhile, Red had pulled her hair high into a rhinestone clasp so her dark curly locks with their glittery red streaks fell over her shoulders in a pretty tumble. And Rapunzel had woven her hair into several braids and then twined them together in an intricate affair that hung down her back. Black and silver flowers were threaded here and there through the pretty blue-streaked braids.

"Why aren't you ready?" Red asked Cinda. Then her eyes fell on the dress and slippers Cinda held in her arms and she gasped. "What happened?"

Rapunzel swiveled to look. "It was those Steps, wasn't it?"

"Yes, but they aren't going to get away with their troublemaking this time!" With a determined look on her face, Cinda headed toward the door that led to the tower staircase.

"Where are you going?" called Snow.

"To the library," said Cinda. "For a new ball gown."

"Wait for us," said Red, as the girls caught up to her. "We'll help you find the goose doorknob."

Snow nodded. "We can split up in pairs to search faster."

"Right," Rapunzel agreed. "And once you have a new dress, we'll all go to the ball together."

"Where we'll foil whatever mischief those horrible stepsisters of yours have planned!" added Red.

Cinda's jaw dropped. She wasn't used to having supportive, kindhearted girlfriends like these. "Are you sure?" she asked uncertainly.

The three girls enveloped her in a group hug. "Of course!" said Red.

"No way we'd leave you behind," said Snow. "It's one for all and all for one."

"That's right!" said Rapunzel. "Why should you have to miss out just because of your mean stepsisters?"

Without another word, the four girls dashed from the dorm.

13

Gown Shopping (Again)

As the girls ran up and down staircases and through hallways looking for the library, they could hear music floating on the air. It was coming from the ball. Where everyone was starting to arrive. And where a dastardly plot would unfold if they weren't there in time to stop it.

Eventually, Cinda and Red found the *GA*-less doorknob on the stairwell wall between the second and third floors. Without thinking, Cinda reached to turn it.

"Hold your honkin' horses!" the knob protested, instantly becoming goose-faced. "Nobody enters without answering —"

"Not another riddle!" Cinda begged. "We're kind of in a hurry!"

But the gooseknob wouldn't listen. "What's black and white and black and white?" it demanded, just as Snow and Rapunzel found the other two girls.

The Grimm girls named off a bunch of black-and-white

things. Piano keys. Raccoons. Penguins. Tuxedos. Salt and pepper. All were wrong.

Rapunzel tried another guess, "A zebra?"

"*Honk!* Good guess, but you're only half right," the gooseknob told her. "Guess again."

The girls named more black-and-white things. Finally, Snow said, "A printed page in a book?"

"Half right again!" said the knob.

They all stared at it and each other, totally confused.

Suddenly, Cinda snapped her fingers. "I know! Is it a printed page in a book with a picture of a zebra on it?" She knew she'd guessed correctly when the carved library door appeared around the knob.

Together, the four Grimm girls entered the library. Only the occasional goose was flying back and forth overhead. And Ms. Goose was nowhere around. She was probably already at the ball, Cinda thought. Spotting the library return, she set the tattered yellow gown and slippers in it.

Then the girls all zipped to the *G* section. When they found the magic mirror again, they didn't waste time trying to enlarge it. Instead, Cinda said to the teeny mirror:

"Mirror, Mirror on the wall,
Please make me a new gown for the b —"

Before she could finish, the magic mirror interrupted her, saying:

"I know what you are going to ask,
But I cannot perform the task.
The rule of mirrors on the wall
Is one gown per girl for any ball."

"Oh, no!" said Red.

"That's not in the handbook," Snow argued.

But the mirror didn't reply. It had apparently said all it was going to say. And that was that.

"What do we do now?" asked Rapunzel.

"Maybe I can convince the knights guarding the Great Hall doors to let me in dressed like this?" suggested Cinda. She peered down at her cloak, seeing the bottom of her pj's and her sneakers sticking out below it.

The others stared at her and shook their heads. "No way," said Red. "Balls have a strict dress code."

"Then you guys should go to the ball without me and do what you can to stop the Steps," Cinda decided. "Meanwhile, I'll go look for another mirror that might help me. I remember seeing a room full of them the other day."

"We're not leaving you," said Red.

"You might need our help," said Snow.

"Yeah, you don't really know your way around. You could get lost in this place for the whole night!" Rapunzel agreed. "C'mon."

Not giving her a chance to argue them out of it, the three girls rushed off toward the *M* section. Cinda zoomed after them, hoping to find a more helpful mirror.

When they entered the *M* section, they heard someone singing. High on a shelf beside her, Cinda saw a sparkly foot-long pink stick with a little starburst at one end. It was doing flips and twirls.

"Wing-a-ling, *zing*! I love-a to sing!" it sang as it whirled and somersaulted.

What was a wand doing in the *M*'s? Cinda wondered. Then she thought of a possible reason. "Are you a *magic* wand?" she asked it.

"Yes!" it replied in a happy voice. It flipped down to a lower shelf on a level with Cinda's shoulders. "Name's LaWanda."

Cinda curtsied as best she could in her pj's and cloak. "Pleased to meet you. I'm Cinderella. Do you think you could lend me enough magic to change my pajamas into a ball gown?"

"What'll you trade?" asked LaWanda.

Cinda and her friends looked at each other.

"Nothing," Cinda admitted. "I mean, we don't have —"

"Okay! I'll trade you my magic for nothing!" said LaWanda. "What a deal I made. Woo-hoo!" The wand did a joyous flip in the air and landed right side up again. "Take off your cloak, please."

What a good-hearted wand, thought Cinda. "Thanks!" she told it, tossing her cloak on a shelf.

Before she could make any suggestions about what kind of gown she'd like, LaWanda decided for her. With a single leap into the air, the wand began spinning around over Cinda's head, raining pink sparkles down on her.

"Presto. Change-o. Here we go-ho!" the wand singsonged.

All at once, Cinda's pj's turned into the most beautiful ball gown she'd ever seen! It was bright white with puffed sleeves and a heart-shaped neckline edged with pearls. Its long, full skirt was covered with a layer of sparkly gauzy stuff that seemed to float around her like a cloud. There was a wide, glossy pink ribbon belted around her waist that fell into a bunch of curly ribbons at the back. White elbow-length gloves completed the outfit.

Red clapped her hands together in delight. "You look beautiful!"

Snow sighed happily. "That dress is *grimmtasmagoric*!"

"What about her hair?" Rapunzel asked the wand.

In response to her question, LaWanda let out a high whistle. Instantly, a dozen bluebirds flew from somewhere across the library, bringing small bags of silver and pink pearls.

With their help, the girls arranged Cinda's hair into long soft waves. Supervised by the wand, the bluebirds tucked glossy silver and pink pearls here and there into her new style. Within minutes, all was done, and the bluebirds fluttered away again.

"Wow! I feel so glamorous," Cinda breathed, giving a little twirl. The gown's skirt swished around her in an elegant way. She looked at LaWanda and the other Grimm girls. "Thank you, thank you, thank you all!"

"Gowns are my specialty," said the wand, sounding pleased with itself.

"How about slippers?" Snow asked.

"There's not enough magic left in me to create slippers," LaWanda admitted. "It'll take me at least an hour to recharge."

"That's okay," Cinda told her. "I'll go look for some in the *S* section."

"Take me with you," begged the wand. "I'll help you choose."

Cinda grabbed LaWanda and her cloak, and the girls zipped through the aisles, their ball gowns rustling. But when they reached the *S* aisle, the shelves were empty, except for the tags.

"Oh! All the slippers have been checked out for the ball!" wailed Snow.

"I'll just go in my sneakers," suggested Cinda. Maybe no one would notice. And if they did, who cared what they thought? Cinda kind of did, actually, but whatever.

The other girls looked doubtful. Still, there didn't seem to be any choice. On their way out of the library, they went through the *G* section. There, they came to a screeching halt.

Because right in the middle of the aisle floor sat a single pair of glittery glass slippers. They scooted themselves up to Cinda and began tap dancing around as if they were trying to impress her. Cinda stared at them in surprise.

"They're perfect!" trilled LaWanda. "Try them on!"

Cinda looked at the wand. She'd forgotten she still held it.

"Look! There are tiny words written inside them," said Snow. She kneeled and read the words from one of the slippers aloud:

"These glass slippers will convey
the magical power to lead the way."

"Maybe they'll lead you to the missing pumpkin so we can give it to the principal," said Red.

"That would spoil your stepsisters' evil plans!" agreed Rapunzel.

Cinda looked at the slippers. "I'm not sure. How could glass slippers be comfortable? I mean, I'm not that great at dancing to begin with. I think I'd better just wear my sneakers."

"No! You can't! Sneakers are not happily-ever-after enough! Try the glass slippers on!" begged LaWanda.

The other girls grinned at Cinda. "You heard her," said Red.

The glass slippers began stepping up their efforts to be chosen, too, performing what appeared to be can-can kicks.

Not wanting to disappoint the helpful wand, her friends, or the slippers, either, Cinda kicked off her sneakers and stepped into the glass shoes. They were small, but luckily, so were her feet. The glass slippers fit her perfectly. She took a couple of steps in them.

"Well?" asked Snow.

"They're comfy. It's almost like being barefoot," said Cinda.

Not only that, the slippers made Cinda feel lighter somehow. Happy. She took a few more steps in them. The steps turned into dance steps, whirling her into a graceful waltz right there in the middle of the aisle. And she wasn't even in the *W* for Waltz section or the *D* for Dance section!

Cinda looked at the others in surprise. "Well, if the slippers' powers will help me to dance better, I'm all for it!"

"Time for you to go-ho have fun!" said LaWanda. The magic wand did a series of flips high in the air. Almost instantly, a goose with a net bag swooped down to carry the wand back to its shelf in the *M* section.

"Thank you!" Cinda called after the departing wand.

"Toodle-ooooo!" LaWanda called back.

Then Cinda and the other three Grimm girls scurried off to the ball in a whoosh of satin and sparkles.

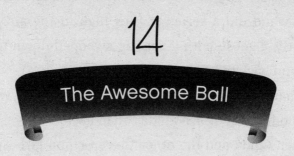

14

The Awesome Ball

As Cinda, Red, Snow, and Rapunzel got closer to the Great Hall, the Hickory Dickory Dock clock bonged out eleven o'clock.

How has so much time passed? wondered Cinda. Then she remembered what the other Grimm girls had told her about library time. How it could speed up or slow down.

"Only one hour until midnight," noted Red.

"I hope we're not too late to derail your stepsisters' plot," said Rapunzel.

Snow nodded. "Let's all split up and keep our eyes open. We can meet at the table at the far end of the Hall when we have something to report." She and the other girls moved ahead and were quickly swallowed up in the crowd.

Unfortunately, the Steps would spot her right away, Cinda thought as she paused at the entrance to the Hall. And that could make it harder to stop their dastardly plan. If only she had some disguise!

Just then, a knight guard reached for the cloak she'd brought to hang it up. He looked surprised when she handed him her sneakers first. As he took the cloak from her as well, something fell from its pocket. The white masketball mask from the game last Monday! She'd stuck it in her cloak pocket, intending to return it to the gym during the week. But she'd gotten so busy, she had forgotten all about it.

Perfect! Quickly, Cinda slipped the mask on.

Tonight she'd be the only one wearing a mask, which would be a little odd. However, it was cute and it did match her dress. And with the masketball mask on, although Cinda would still look like herself, no one would recognize her! Including the Steps and any of their Evil Society friends who might be lurking.

The moment Cinda entered the ballroom, heads turned to stare at her. "Who is that beautiful girl?" she heard someone whisper. It was really the ball gown they were admiring, she decided. It was so grimmazing that anyone would look beautiful in it.

The boys especially were looking at her in a way she wasn't used to. Almost like they were in awe of her! Though none of them came up to her, they bowed low and cleared a path before her. It made her feel weird. Especially since these were some of the same guys she'd played a rough-and-tumble game of masketball with last Monday.

Cinda gazed at the transformed Great Hall in wonder. Huge swags of white satin hung around each window, all of which had been left open to let in the cool night air. The two long meal tables had been removed. Instead, smaller satin-draped tables sat here and there with white chairs tucked around them. Each table had snacks and party favors, plus a glorious bouquet in the middle.

And amid each flowery centerpiece was — a little pumpkin! The pumpkins had been decorated to look like small fanciful coaches drawn by tiny white toy horses. Oh, no! If Peter Peter's pumpkin *was* here, how were she and her friends ever going to find it among so many other pumpkins?

Almost immediately, Cinda spotted both Steps over by one of the tables. They were talking to Prince Awesome. Were they trying to recruit him for that Evil Society they'd mentioned? Cinda slipped over to stand behind them, where she could listen in.

"How positively E.V.I.L!" she heard Malorette say to the prince. She spoke each letter clearly, as if they were initials.

"If you say so," said Awesome.

Grinning prettily, Malorette tapped him with her fan in a teasing way. "So about that dance?" she hinted.

"It would be my pleasure," the prince replied in a formal voice, offering her his arm. As he swept Malorette off to the dance floor, Odette turned toward the snack table and Cinda. Her eyes grew envious as they swept over Cinda's gown.

"What's up with that mask?" she asked.

"It's just for fun," said Cinda. She held her breath. Would Odette see through her disguise? No. She didn't seem to recognize her at all!

Pretending she was only there for a snack, Cinda picked up a cupcake from the table. It had pink frosting and a cute little crown made of sugar on top. She took a quick bite.

"May I have this dance?" a tremulous voice asked her. Foulsmell had come up to stand beside her.

"Ur, no, thernk you," she told him around a mouthful of cupcake. She looked over her shoulder. Odette had disappeared. And she couldn't see Awesome or Malorette among the dancers. Nor Red, Snow, or Rapunzel!

"Sure. Okay. You don't have to. I understand." Foulsmell stuck his hands in his pockets and started sidling away. His cheeks had gone as pink as the cupcake frosting when she'd turned him down.

Oh, boppingfangle! Cinda did not have time for this. But she wasn't going to leave poor Foulsmell feeling rejected and embarrassed.

"Wait." She set down the half-eaten cupcake and lifted her mask just a little, so he could see it was her. "It's me, Cinda," she whispered. "The reason I said no just now is because I stink at dancing. I only came here tonight because I'm on a mission. Have you seen Red? Or Snow or Rapunzel?"

"I think so," Foulsmell said, not asking about the mask or the mission. Wasn't he the least bit curious? He seemed to accept things for what they were without worrying about whether they were strange or not — like his own name. "I saw them on the other side of the Hall," he added. "I could dance you over there?"

"Okay," Cinda said reluctantly. She really didn't want to hurt his feelings, but she didn't want to hurt his feet, either. Still, dancing might be the quickest way to reach her friends.

At her agreement, Foulsmell's face brightened and he took her gloved hand. They whirled around the dance floor to the other side of the room. The crossover happened so fast and smoothly, Cinda hardly even realized she'd been dancing. Somehow, the slippers had made it easy for her!

"Thought you said you couldn't dance," said Foulsmell, grinning at her.

"I can't. It's these glass slippers that can," she said breathlessly. "Wait, my friends are right over there. Okay if we stop?"

"Sure," he said. After they halted, Foulsmell bowed to her. Then he walked off, looking proud of himself for having been the first to ask Cinda — or the strange masked girl — to dance.

Cinda scurried over to Red, Snow, and Rapunzel. "Psst!" she told them. "Any luck?" Not recognizing her, they just looked at her in surprise.

"It's me, Cinda," she said, lifting a corner of her mask.

At that, their faces lit up. "Finally!" Red exclaimed.

"Where've you been?" asked Snow.

"And why the mask?" asked Rapunzel. Unlike Foulsmell, her new friends were the curious types. Like she was!

"Later," Cinda said quickly. "What do you guys actually know about the Evil Society?"

The three girls shrugged.

"Nothing, really," said Red.

"Until you told us your stepsisters mentioned it, I'd never even heard of it," said Rapunzel.

Snow nodded. "Same here."

"I think it might be an acronym, as in E.V.I.L.," Cinda explained. "You know, where each letter stands for something?"

"You mean like Edible Vacations In Lollipopland?" joked Red. They all giggled.

Then Rapunzel suggested, "Or how about Extra Vain Itchy Ladies?"

Now they were all laughing really hard. Including Cinda. But then suddenly her three friends fell silent. They were looking at something behind her. Or someone.

Cinda turned to see Prince Awesome. He was wearing black boots so polished she could see herself in them, as well as a fancy vest over a white shirt, trousers, and a jacket with tails. He definitely looked . . . well, awesome!

"May I have this dance?" he asked Cinda politely. She could tell by his stiffness that he didn't recognize her.

She knew him, though, obviously. "No, thank you," she blurted.

The prince stared at Cinda as if stunned. His cheeks flushed just a little. Was he embarrassed? Like Foulsmell had been? Prince Awesome was rich, handsome, and good at sports. Probably no one had ever said no to him when he'd asked them to dance before. Was it possible that the one thing his tutors hadn't prepared him for was rejection? In that moment, Cinda kind of felt sorry for him.

Red elbowed her. It was impolite to refuse a dance with the host of the ball. Even Cinda knew that. But her dance with Foulsmell might have been a lucky fluke. She didn't want to make a fool of herself with Awesome and embarrass him more than she already had. Or embarrass *herself* either. Although very few people knew who she was, others might somehow figure it out. Or guess later!

"It's not you —" she began. Then Cinda stopped. She'd just spotted her two Steps across the room, staring at the floor. What they were up to? *Hmm.*

Prince Awesome cocked his head at her, waiting for her to finish. Dancing seemed to be the fastest way to get around in here. And she really wanted to know what the Steps were up to.

Cinda turned her blue eyes up to meet the prince's dazzling brown ones. "Actually, I'd love to dance with you."

She placed a white-gloved hand on the arm he offered. *Come on, glass slippers. Don't fail me now*, she thought as Prince Awesome swept her out onto the dance floor.

After a few seconds, she realized that nothing terrible had happened. She was actually dancing! Usually, she was awkward, clumsy, and stepping offbeat to the music. But now she was swaying and gliding and swooping just like all the other dancers. As if she knew what she was doing. Or more like the *glass slippers* did!

Cinda looked toward the place where she'd seen the Steps. The spot where she'd hoped to head. They weren't there anymore! As she whirled and twirled, she peered over the prince's shoulder, trying to find them again.

"Do I know you?" the prince asked her.

"Doubt it," she told him, not paying much attention as her eyes searched the Hall. Then she looked up at him and added, "Sorry. That was kind of rude."

But Awesome just laughed. "It's okay if you want to stay incognito."

Cinda grinned, relaxing a bit at his casual attitude. And then — just when she'd stopped worrying about her dancing, her glass slippers began acting weird. They took her left. Then they marched her right. They jerked her this way and that.

The slippers' tag had said they liked to "lead." Now it appeared they'd decided to do precisely that!

Unable to help herself, Cinda pulled the prince along with her as the slippers wove them through the crowd willy-nilly. "Sorry! Excuse me!" she called as she bumped into people. When they suddenly came upon the Steps, Cinda accidentally bumped into them extra hard, sending the two girls falling over in heaps of satin and silk.

Without giving her time to apologize, the slippers lurched off and danced Cinda and the prince in the opposite direction, toward a window. But before they could reach it, Cinda tripped over one of the stone floor tiles.

"Whoa!" said the prince. He grabbed at her arm to keep her from falling.

"I'm so sorry!" she told him breathlessly. "Maybe that's enough dancing for now."

But her slippers had other ideas, and swept them both off into the crowd again. They were out of control! As Cinda and the prince whirled around the dance floor, unable to stop, the slippers kept "leading" them back to the same stone tile she had tripped over.

The third time she stepped on it, she noticed that the tile was loose. Hey! Were the glass slippers trying to tell her something? she wondered. What if the pumpkin was hidden under the tile!

Just then, the grandfather clock woke up.

"Hickory Dickory Dock,
The mouse ran up the clock.
It's twelve midnight.
This ball's over, quite.
Hickory Dickory Dock."

As the mechanical mouse began to squeak, the little sparkles on Cinda's dress began to pop off. *Ping! Ping! Ping!* What was happening? she wondered in alarm.

Then Cinda remembered. Everyone else's gowns had special permission to be out past midnight. But she hadn't properly checked out the gown *she* was wearing. Even if LaWanda had conjured it up instead of the magic mirror, it must be due back in the library at midnight.

Or else.

Cinda had a sneaky feeling she was about to find out what the phrase "dire consequences" meant. She glanced past the prince toward the exit. She had a choice. She could flee so no one would see whatever dire thing was going to happen.

Or she could stay, regardless of the consequences to herself, and lift that loose floor tile to check and see if the pumpkin was hidden there. She wouldn't put it past the Steps to have cast a spell on it to explode on the last stroke of midnight and bewitch the prince into liking them, or worse . . . make him want to join their Evil Society!

Coming to a decision, Cinda excused herself to the prince, ducked through the dancers, dashed to the tile, and moved it aside. As she'd suspected, there was something under it. But to her surprise, it was *not* a pumpkin.

Instead, as the Hickory Dickory mouse finished squeaking and the clock began to bong, Cinda pulled a two-foot long cylindrical object wrapped in several layers of vellum paper from underneath the tile. When she pulled back a corner of the vellum she saw that the object was actually some kind of rolled-up rug or tapestry.

Was this what the slippers wanted her to find? What about the "big pumpkin rollout"? Hadn't the Steps said that was supposed to happen tonight? Cinda tried to remember their exact words, but with those bongs sounding in her ears, she was panicking, unable to think clearly.

Bong! As the clock struck its final bong she leaped to her feet. It was now officially midnight. Suddenly, the dress she was wearing began shooting sparkles in every direction. *Ping! Pingety-ping! Whrrrr! Phewww!* It was giving off fireworks!

Horribly embarrassed, Cinda clutched the paper-wrapped tapestry tight and raced for the Great Hall door that led to Pink Castle. About halfway across the Hall, however, she glimpsed the Steps in the act of plucking a pumpkin coach from a bouquet centerpiece.

"Aha!" she called. "Caught you!"

She veered their way, yanking the little pumpkin coach from Malorette's hands. She had only the merest glimpse of her Steps' shocked expressions, because the glass slippers chose that moment to lead Cinda into a fancy spin. Tripping, she accidentally lobbed the tiny pumpkin coach in a high arc. As if she'd shot for a goal in a masketball game, it sailed overhead. And . . . right . . . out . . . of . . . the . . . window into the black night.

Splash! At the very instant the pumpkin hit the Once Upon River down below, Cinda's gown turned back into her pj's.

All around her, there was now dead silence. Even the musicians had stopped playing. She peeked over her shoulder and saw that everyone — including the prince and the Steps — had been watching. They'd seen every embarrassing thing that had just happened!

Mortified, Cinda dashed off again, still holding the wrapped rug-thing. As she flew through the door, she remembered that she still had her mask on. *Hurrah!* With the exception of her Grimm girl friends and Foulsmell, no one else would know who she was.

Giving up on trying to retrieve the pumpkin — it was too dark outside to find it now — Cinda left the Hall. She ran for the grand winding staircase in Pink Castle, and started up it. She didn't want to risk being unmasked by the Steps or Prince Awesome right now!

Unfortunately, she was in such a hurry that partway up, she caught her heel and stumbled. Cinda grabbed at the railing to keep herself from falling and watched help- lessly as one of her slippers tumbled back down the stairs. Hearing footsteps behind her, she began to race upward again, leaving the slipper behind.

15

Perfect Fit

The next morning, Cinda woke just in time to see Mermily tiptoeing into their room. Where did that girl sleep? Not in her bed, that was for sure. It was still neatly made. Maybe in the fountain?

Cinda pretended to still be asleep but watched from barely open eyes as Mermily grabbed a dress from her armoire, then tiptoed back out. Probably to the washroom.

When she was gone again, Cinda pulled the single glass slipper out from under her pillow. She'd tucked it under there last night to keep it near. Because, in spite of the disastrous way the night had ended, the slippers had made her feel magical. For a while, she'd felt the complete opposite of a Loserella. She'd felt beautiful. She'd even been able to dance! Too bad she had to return the slippers today. Both of them.

Cinda wasn't looking forward to asking Prince Awesome for the other one. Her Grimm girl friends — Red and Snow, anyway — had followed her upstairs soon after she'd fled last night. (Rapunzel had stayed behind due to her fear of heights, but also to check the river for any sign of the pumpkin.) Red had retrieved her cloak and sneakers, but had told her that the prince had picked up the other slipper after Cinda had fled.

Would Cinda's library borrowing privileges be taken away for losing the white gown, and for having returned the yellow gown and slippers in tatters? And for not checking out the glass slippers? She wasn't looking forward to explaining to Ms. Goose about all *that*, either.

Sticking a hand under her mattress, Cinda felt around for the tapestry she'd found in the Hall the night before. It was there, safely tucked where she'd hidden it. She, Red, and Snow had tried to unroll it after the ball. That had proven impossible. Tired, they'd given up and agreed to try again with Rapunzel this morning. But first, all four girls had to return their borrowed stuff to the library.

"Cinda?" It was Red's voice outside the curtain.

"I'm up," said Cinda. "Be ready in a jiff."

" 'Kay," said Red.

A few minutes later, Cinda, Red, and Snow met up with Rapunzel on the first floor, and headed for the Grimmstone Library. Some other girls in Pearl Tower who'd already returned their gowns had told them its door was located near Mr. Hump-Dumpty's class today.

"I checked the river again this morning for that pumpkin," Rapunzel informed them as they walked. "Nothing."

"Maybe it sank," said Snow.

Rapunzel shook her head. "Pumpkins are full of air. They float. Maybe it was swept downriver."

"I guess there's no way we'll ever know for certain if it was Peter Peter's missing pumpkin," said Red.

Cinda was quiet the whole way down the hall, worrying about that. She went over in her mind what she'd overheard the Steps say the day before in their dorm alcove. They must have hidden the pumpkin in one of the centerpieces before the ball. But why? What had they been planning to do with it? And by accidentally tossing the pumpkin out the window, had Cinda spoiled their plan . . . or helped them? It was all so confusing.

The four girls met lots of other students on their way to the library. Girls carrying ball gowns and slippers. Boys toting classy tuxedos and shiny shoes. The only thing Cinda had with her was a single glass slipper tucked in the bag she'd brought.

"I'll meet you there," Cinda told her friends. Then she split off, going to look for the prince so she could ask for her other slipper back.

Out in the herb garden, some students were sitting on benches and stone walls. Foulsmell was playing a game of quoits on the lawn. He waved when he saw her and she waved back.

The Steps were there, too. They must've already turned

in their ball stuff, because they were hanging out with some girls from Ruby Tower, doing a complicated game of magic jump rope. As Cinda passed, the Steps murmured a new rhyme just loud enough for her to hear:

"Cinderella, hair all yella,
You should do what your sisters tell ya.
Too bad you couldn't go to the ball,
Because your gown was torn and all."

The two girls high-fived mid-jump, then started laughing.

Ooh! They made Cinda so-o mad! She'd have the last laugh, though, because she *had* gone to the ball. They just didn't know it — yet.

Right at that moment, Prince Awesome entered the garden. He was cradling the other glass slipper in both hands! Going up to the first girl he saw, he presented the shoe to her. Cinda couldn't hear what he said, but the girl immediately kicked off one of her shoes and tried on the slipper.

When it didn't fit her, Cinda watched as the prince moved on to several more girls. Some of them refused to try on the slipper, but many more were willing. Excitement began to grow as everyone wondered why the prince was searching for a girl who could wear the slipper.

As more and more girls tried on the glittery glass shoe,

Cinda wondered what the problem was. The slippers weren't all *that* small. Were they magically resizing themselves so no one could wear them?

She was too embarrassed to go ask the prince to give her the slipper with everyone watching. That would be the same as admitting that she'd been the one making a fool of herself on the dance floor last night. That concern didn't stop the Steps, though.

They eagerly ran over and took a turn. Malorette sat on the edge of the garden fountain and batted her eyelashes at the prince as she tried to ram her foot into the slipper. No go. Not one to give up easily, Malorette huffed and puffed and pushed, her face turning red. It didn't do her any good, though. The slipper still wouldn't fit.

"Let me try," said Odette, shoving her aside.

Splash! In her excitement, Odette toppled Malorette into the fountain. Or had the *slipper* caused it to happen? Either way, when she came out, the girl was drenched. And angry.

"It was an accident!" Odette wailed. But Malorette didn't seem to think so. The sopping-wet girl flew after her sister, hurling insults. Forgetting about trying on the slipper, Odette took off across the garden. Cinda couldn't help grinning. She wanted to leave before the prince got around to her. Still, she hesitated. She needed to return *both* slippers to the library.

Before she could decide what to do, the mischievous

glass slipper suddenly sprang from the prince's hands and started clomping across a bed of clover toward her. Cinda's eyes widened. Without stopping to think, she raced from the garden. But the slipper followed. *Tap! Tap!*

"Wait up!" called the prince. He caught up to her in the hall at the exact same time that her lost slipper did. The matching slipper leaped from her bag down to the floor to join its twin. Both slippers began twirling on their toes and doing dance steps, as if begging her to try them on again.

Although she was more than a little embarrassed, Cinda couldn't help chuckling at their antics. Relenting at last, she kicked off her sneakers. "Sorry I left you behind last night," she told the lost glass slipper. Then she slid both slippers on. They fit perfectly, of course.

She glanced up at the prince. "I don't suppose you could forget that you saw me in my pj's at the ball last night," she said.

He cocked his head, pretending to be confused. "Pj's? What pj's?" he teased. "All I remember is a lovely girl in a beautiful white dress who danced like a dream."

Cinda heard some girls nearby sigh happily. Because that was a really sweet thing for a guy to say. She opened her mouth, unsure what she was going to reply. The words that came out surprised her.

"Be careful," she told the prince in an undertone too soft for anyone else to hear. "I think something's afoot in this academy."

He grinned at her, then gestured toward her slippered foot. "That was a joke, right?"

"No. I mean it," she said, keeping her voice low. "Something's *afoot,* as in something's not quite right. You're new at the school, too, so I know you can't be involved. I only wanted to warn you to not join any evil societies or anything. And to just . . . be careful."

Prince Awesome tucked his hands in his pockets and stared at her in a puzzled way. Did he think she was twaddle-brained for saying all that? It *had* sounded kind of strange.

"Well, thanks for giving me back my slipper," Cinda said at last. She tried to kick the slippers off again. When they refused to budge, she simply put her sneakers in her bag and turned away, intending to follow a group of students carrying fancy gowns and tunics.

"Cinda?" Prince Awesome called to her.

She looked back at him.

"There's a pickup masketball game on Monday after school in the Grimm Gym. We're starting teams. Practices will be sixth period, so if we make the team, we'll automatically get permission to switch from Balls to Gym," he said. "You in?"

Cinda's face broke into a huge smile. "Double, triple *definitely*!" This was the best news she'd had all morning. All week, maybe!

The smile the prince beamed back at her made Cinda's insides feel all funny. In a good way, though.

"Cool. See you later, then," Awesome called. Whistling, he walked off.

As she watched him go, Cinda remembered that she might not be here long enough to make the team. If she got expelled for any of the mistakes she'd made, that is. She hoped she wouldn't!

When she arrived at the Grimmstone Library, the door was already propped open. So, thankfully, no one had to answer any gooseknob riddles.

"Good. You got the other slipper," said Red as Cinda joined her friends in a long line to wait for Ms. Goose to check in their borrowed finery.

Seeing that Snow had brought her vellum book reminded Cinda of something she wanted to look up. She asked to borrow it.

"Sure," said Snow. "But it'll only respond to my voice commands. Which class do you want?"

"History, please," Cinda replied.

"Grimm History of Beasts and Dastardlies," Snow told the book as she pressed a finger to the oval on its cover. Then she handed the book to Cinda, while Red took charge of Cinda's sneakers.

As the line moved slowly forward, Cinda thumbed

through endless pages. Realizing she wasn't finding what she wanted, she finally tried the index. Under *E*, there was an entry that caught her eye: *E.V.I.L. Society.*

"Look!" Cinda cried softly. She turned the book so the other three girls could see.

Snow reached out and pressed her fingertip over the *E.V.I.L.* letters. Instantly, a small, clear bubble rose to hover a few inches above the page. Inside it, a definition was printed in small type: *Exceptional Villains In Literature.*

Cinda's eyes widened. So that's what the acronym stood for!

Snow read the rest of the definition in a soft voice. " 'A secret society bent on evil. Established in the Dark Ages. Now defunct.' "

Pop! After Snow finished reading, the bubble popped on its own and disappeared.

A shiver zipped up Cinda's spine. "Could E.V.I.L. be the foe Ms. Jabberwocky was talking about?" she exclaimed in a whisper. "The one that has the principal worried?"

"But the book says it's defunct. No longer in existence," said Red.

"What if someone has started it up again?" asked Rapunzel.

With worried eyes, they all stared at one another. No one had an answer to that!

16

Magic Charm

Just then, the Grimm girls reached the front of the line. Snow closed the vellum book and tucked it in the crook of her arm. Ms. Goose quickly checked in the gowns and slippers the other three girls had brought back. Then it was Cinda's turn.

When Cinda explained about the ripped yellow gown and slippers she'd already returned, Ms. Goose was naturally upset. However, when Cinda also mentioned the missing white gown and started to explain that she'd forgotten to check it out, Ms. Goose interrupted her.

"Let me see." The librarian studied her list. "Ah, yes, your white gown brought itself back last night. I discovered it this morning in the Lost and Found bin with your yellow outfit. At midnight, any late artifacts usually go a bit haywire — or a lot haywire — then pop themselves back to the library of their own accord. Unless they've gotten trapped somehow, that is."

Her words sparked an idea in Cinda's mind. "What if an artifact *was* trapped somewhere, though?" she asked.

Catching on quickly, Red added, "You mean, like in a trunker?"

"That could certainly prevent an artifact from making its way into the Lost and Found," said Ms. Goose.

The missing pumpkin had been trapped in her trunker last Monday, Cinda thought. But where was it now? Downriver? Or had the Steps found it floating in the river before Rapunzel had looked for it? Or maybe that pumpkin she'd tossed out of the Hall last night wasn't even the right pumpkin at all!

Cinda's thoughts were like a jumble of mismatched stockings. She dared not go to the principal about all this without more evidence against the Steps. Plus, none of them knew who might be part of E.V.I.L.

"Let's see," mused Ms. Goose. "One ruined gown and slippers. Another gown left to find its way back to the library on its own." The librarian got out an abacus and started doing calculations.

"Oh, I almost forgot," Cinda added. Reluctantly, she removed the slippers, which slid right off her feet this time.

As she set them in the library return box on the desk, Ms. Goose checked her list again. "Hmm. I don't have any record of glass slippers being checked out. No record of them at all, in fact. Those slippers don't belong in the Grimmstone Library."

"But I got them here last night," said Cinda.

"Nonsense," Ms. Goose said briskly. She glanced at her abacus again. "Looks like you've earned yourself three demerits. And a note about this incident must go home to your family."

"Oh, no!" Cinda said. Hearing snickers behind her, she glanced over her shoulder. The Steps had apparently come along to witness her punishment for the trouble *they'd* made, just for fun.

"That's not really fair," Red blurted out. "Because she's not the one who ruined the dress and slippers last night."

Ms. Goose tilted her head, causing her glasses to slip to the end of her nose. She glanced down at the library return box. "Well, then, who did?" she asked.

Cinda and the three Grimm girls just looked at one another. They knew exactly who'd done it, but they couldn't prove it. And Cinda was reluctant to rat out her stepsisters to Ms. Goose, even if they did deserve it. "I don't think I —" she began.

"I wasn't asking you," Ms. Goose interrupted. "I was asking the glass slippers. They seem to want to tell us something." And indeed, the slippers were hopping up and down inside the library return, as if bursting with determination to get in on the conversation.

"What?" Cinda asked blankly.

As if in answer, the glass slippers eagerly leaped out of the library return and clomped over to Malorette and Odette. Everyone in line moved back to watch as the slippers proceeded to point their toes at the Steps, making little kicking motions. It was like they were accusing them!

"Aha!" said Ms. Goose. "Malorette and Odette of Grimm, you are guilty of destroying library property. You will receive two demerits each and a note will go home to your parents."

The Steps' jaws dropped.

"But —" Malorette sputtered.

"Wait —" Odette blustered.

"Oops! Make that three demerits each," Ms. Goose corrected. "Because Cinderella would not have borrowed her white gown from the library if you hadn't destroyed her yellow gown in the first place. Furthermore, you will do scullery duty with Mistress Hagscorch for two weeks, starting today."

The Steps' eyes widened in alarm. Looked like Cinda and Snow weren't the only ones who found the Academy's cook a bit scary.

Then Ms. Goose turned to Cinda. "You, on the other hand, are the innocent party here, and will receive no punishment."

Thinking that Cinda's business was finished now, some other students in line behind her and her friends stepped up. Stunned, Cinda moved out of their way. "What about the glass slippers?" she remembered to ask the librarian.

"They are obviously a magical charm, not an artifact," Ms. Goose informed her. "Now run along. And take the slippers with you."

Malorette and Odette must have heard what Ms. Goose said, because now their look of alarm changed to one that was positively green with envy.

"You got a charm? Already?" Red said in delight as they left the library.

"It's an honor to be chosen by a charm so soon after you've arrived," said Snow. "Most students go to school for months or years before it happens. None of us has been chosen yet."

Cinda clutched the glittery glass slippers tight. "So I can keep them?" She hadn't dared to hope that might be possible.

Her friends nodded.

"They've got magical powers only you can unlock," said Rapunzel. "That's how charms work."

"Wow!" said Cinda, gazing at the slippers in wonder as she put them on.

"Take care," Snow warned. "Some students will be jealous." She nodded toward the Steps, who were stalking away down the hall.

Cinda lifted her chin. Too bad for them. Her dad was going to hear about the trouble they'd made soon enough. Then he'd realize that the Steps weren't so sweet, after all. Cinda didn't suppose for one minute that they'd tell her dad about her getting a charm, however. They only liked to tell him bad stuff about her. Stuff they mainly made up. She smiled to herself. She'd tell him, though, as soon as she got the chance!

Later, after breakfast in the Great Hall, Mermily was outside working on the fountain again. So the Grimm girls gathered in Cinda's room in Pearl Tower to make another attempt to open the rolled tapestry.

This time they tried all kinds of magical passwords and spells, in addition to just plain pushing and pulling at it. Nothing worked. They were about to give up, when the tapestry suddenly leaped from their hands into the middle of the floor, where it unrolled itself.

"Whoa!" Cinda exclaimed. "What made that happen?"

Red shook her head. "No clue."

The girls got on their hands and knees and gathered around to examine the two-foot square piece of cloth.

"What is it?" asked Rapunzel, turning her head this way and that to view it from every angle.

"A map!" declared Cinda. "It's Grimmlandia. See?" She pointed out various familiar landmarks like the Academy itself and London Bridge. "It seems to be unfinished in places. Especially around the edges."

Snow tapped a finger to her chin, thinking hard. "You know what? I think this is actually a mapestry — a magical map in the form of a stitched tapestry."

"A mapestry?" Rapunzel arched an eyebrow. "But those are supposed to lead to —"

"Hidden objects," finished Red.

"Or treasure," added Snow. Her eyes sparkled with excitement. "Have you ever heard that old legend about an ancient treasure being hidden somewhere in Grimmlandia?"

Red and Rapunzel nodded.

"I haven't. What kind of treasure?" asked Cinda.

"No one knows," said Red.

"Look!" Rapunzel's dark eyes went wide and she pointed at a long bright-blue section of the mapestry — Once Upon River. "Something's happening! See that embroidered orange blob?"

"Yeah. It wasn't there a second ago," said Snow, getting excited, too.

"It just now stitched itself on top of the river!" said Red.

"And now it's moving!" Cinda's voice rose as she spoke until her last syllable turned into a squeak.

The girls watched in amazement as the sewn blob picked up speed, moving away from the river and the Academy, which were at the center of the map.

"What if it's . . . *real*!" breathed Cinda. "What if that orange blob is Peter Peter's pumpkin — the same one I tossed into the river last night? And what if it's really moving along the path shown here?"

"C'mon!" said Red. Grabbing the mapestry, she dashed through the curtain and the common room to the outside walkway between Pearl and Ruby towers. The other girls raced after her.

"There!" said Rapunzel. She pointed to something in the distance, while at the same time staying well away from the edge of the walkway. Her height phobia again, thought Cinda.

Sure enough, the girls could see something round and orange rolling down a path, moving away from the Academy toward the forest.

"It's a runaway pumpkin!" said Snow.

"Or a pumpkin rollout! Like my stepsisters said," Cinda added. "And the mapestry is tracking its path!"

Suddenly, the pumpkin plunged into Neverwood Forest. As it did, it began growing larger, until it had turned into a full-size beautiful carriage with orange wheels, pulled by four green-and-orange-striped horses. Cinda could just make out a big scrolly *P* on the carriage door.

"That's the pumpkin from the ball last night!" she exclaimed. "The centerpieces were decorated exactly that way."

"It's Peter Peter Pumpkineater's pumpkin for sure, then," said Rapunzel. "I remember he turned it into a carriage exactly like that on Career Day!"

"But Ms. Goose said that library artifacts must never leave the Academy grounds," said Cinda. "What happens if one does? Something worse than dire consequences?"

The three wide-eyed girls nodded. "*Super-duper* dire consequences," they said in unison.

"Like what?" asked Cinda.

"I don't know. I don't think it's ever happened before," said Red.

The girls watched the carriage until they could no longer glimpse it between the trees. Then they all looked down at the map. The stitched blob was still moving.

"It's headed for the wall!" Rapunzel said in horror. They all held their breath, fearing what would happen when the blob hit the wall that surrounded Grimmlandia.

All at once, the orange blob disappeared! It had gone off the edge of the mapestry altogether.

The girls looked up from the map and gazed out over the landscape that stretched into the distance. "Where did it go?" Red asked.

Snow's face was paler than ever. "Into the Nothing-terror," she whispered.

Seeing something move from the corner of her eye, Cinda looked over to see the Steps standing at a window in Ruby Tower next door. They'd been watching the pumpkin roll away, too!

"Quick, hide the mapestry. Take it inside," Cinda told the others. "I'll be right back."

With that, she stomped into Ruby Tower and over to the Steps. "You stole that pumpkin and stuck it in my trunker before school last Monday, didn't you?"

"Yeah," blurted Odette. "But we didn't know it would turn out to be your trunker until —" Malorette elbowed her in the ribs, and Odette clammed up.

"Aha! So you did steal the pumpkin!" said Cinda. "And you somehow magicked it out of there when I wasn't looking. Right before I shut my trunker door. Did you use one of those one hundred percent invisibility spells or something?"

Malorette just smirked. "I don't know what you're talking about. And you can't prove anything. As usual." She and Odette pushed past Cinda and began walking away.

Cinda followed them to their alcove, refusing to give up. "I overheard you talking about a 'pumpkin rollout.' And the E.V.I.L. Society."

Malorette sniffed, and fluffed her poofy black hair. "We don't know anything about that."

"But if such an intriguing society *did* start up again, I know plenty of students and even some teachers here who might be interested in joining it," said Odette, with an identical sniff and fluff. "Maybe some already have."

"Yeah, villainous characters get a bad rap here at the Academy. It's not fair!" Malorette added. "They're just as important in the Books of Grimm as anyone else."

At that moment, Cinda noticed the key dangling from Malorette's necklace. Why was it bone white instead of iron like everyone else's trunker key? she wondered as before. She drew in a sharp breath. "A skeleton key!" she blurted. "Those can open many different locks. That's how you got the pumpkin into and out of my trunker, isn't it?"

"You're talking nonsense," said Malorette. But she and Odette looked nervous now.

From their reactions, it was obvious the Steps were heavily involved in whatever evil stuff was going on around here. Cinda didn't need to hear any more. She turned to go back to Pearl Tower.

"Wait — where are you going?" asked Malorette, sounding a little worried.

"To hang out with my friends," Cinda told her and Odette. "My new, *nice* friends. And you know what? That was *me* at the ball wearing those glass slippers. Me dancing with Prince Awesome. And tomorrow when you're doing scullery duty in Mistress Hagscorch's kitchen, I'll be hanging out with *him* in the gym. Isn't that absolutely grimmtastically grimm*azing*?"

Leaving both Steps with their mouths hanging open in shock, Cinda flounced off to her tower, smiling all the way there.

17

Happily Ever Afternoon

On Sunday, Cinda and her friends decided to have a picnic in the Bouquet Garden to celebrate Cinda's first week at the Academy. They also planned to discuss who else might be involved in the E.V.I.L. Society, to decide who they could trust with their suspicions regarding the missing pumpkin, and to study the mapestry for clues to a possible treasure.

However, when Cinda went to her dorm room before going to meet the others, she discovered a big trunk sitting in the middle of the floor. There was a letter lying on top of it addressed to her. She unfolded it and read:

My dearest daughter Cinda,

I'm sorry I wasn't home to say good-bye before you left for Grimm Academy. I meant to be home to give you this trunk to take with you, but your stepmother had told me school didn't start until next week. Must have been some mistake.

Not likely! thought Cinda. Her stepmom had probably told him that on purpose, to make sure he wouldn't be there to see her off to school! She read on.

I hope you are doing well at the Academy. Your mother would be so proud of you. I am, too. Please enjoy this finery, my beautiful girl.
Love,
Your Dad

Flipping the lock, Cinda opened the trunk.

It was full of dresses! New, fancy ones — a dozen or more. And petticoats, stockings, and slippers, too!

"Wow!" she breathed. All these were for her?

Tears filled Cinda's blue eyes as she examined each article of clothing. Her dad had sent her this gift? It must mean that he hadn't forgotten her, after all. He did care about her!

At the bottom of the trunk, Cinda found the best gift of all. Her father had sent her a framed picture of himself. She lifted it out and stared at his dear face. "Thank you," she whispered. Giving the picture a quick kiss, she set it on her desk next to the one of her mom.

She could hardly wait to write a letter to thank him. And to tell him about the glass slippers charm, last night's ball, her hope of making the new masketball team, and about her teachers and classes. And most especially about her new Grimm girl friends!

Oops! Her friends! They were waiting for her in the garden! There wasn't time to hang everything up now, so Cinda laid the clothing back inside the trunk and shut it. Then she ran out of the room. Realizing she'd forgotten the mapestry, she skidded to a halt and ran back to get it.

She was in such a hurry that she dropped it on the way out again, and the mapestry unrolled. As she started to roll it back up, she noticed something new. A cross-stitched *X* sewn in golden thread had appeared on the map in the center of Neverwood Forest! An *X*-marks-the-spot for treasure, maybe?

Whoa! Wait until the others see this! Quickly, Cinda rolled the mapestry up again, shoved it in a bag and dashed down the twisty stairs with it.

She felt incredibly light on her feet. So happy! It must be the glass slippers. Without them, she probably wouldn't feel so . . . un*loser*ish.

Then Cinda remembered — she wasn't wearing the slippers! She'd put on her sneakers since she'd be tromping through the garden grass. Maybe it was just this pretty day that was making her feel happy. Or the fact that she had interesting classes, had been chosen by magical charmed slippers, and had made new friends.

Not to mention the fact that she had a secret crush. One that she hadn't even admitted to her friends yet: Prince Awesome, of course!

Ever since the ball on Friday, he'd been paying even more attention to her. Did that mean he liked her? Cinda wasn't sure, and she had other, bigger things to deal with at the moment.

Like foiling an E.V.I.L. Society! And figuring out what kind of threat it posed to Grimm Academy. And deciding if that eyeball she thought she'd seen in the Grimm brothers' wing of the library had something to do with all of this.

Seeing Red, Snow, and Rapunzel in the small garden gazebo up ahead, Cinda waved, eager to discuss these matters with her new friends.

"Be right there," she called.

As she zipped down the stone steps into the Bouquet Garden, Cinda heard the School Board helmet-heads make an announcement that rang through the school:

"Attention, all Grimm Academy students! We hope your first week of this term has been a good one. Please have a happily ever afternoon!"

Yes, Cinda thought with a smile. *I definitely will!*

Red Riding Hood is thrilled to try out for the school play. Acting is her dream, and she's great at it — too bad she has stage fright! After a grimmiserable audition, Red decides to focus on helping her friends Cinda, Snow, and Rapunzel save Grimm Academy from the E.V.I.L. Society. But when Red gets lost in Neverwood Forest and runs into Wolfgang, who might be part of E.V.I.L., she needs her magic basket and a grimmazingly dramatic performance to figure out what's going on!